Town at the Top

Town at the Top

by Khadija Buckland

Introduction by Ray Hardman
Chairman of Swindon Town F.C.

Sponsored by Burmah Petroleum Fuels.

A Red House Publication
ISBN 0 9522519 1 4

AUTHOR'S ACKNOWLEDGEMENTS

TOWN at at the Top wouldn't have been possible without help from a man at the top – Rikki Hunt, Managing Director of Burmah Petroleum Fuels.

His endless advice as well as the financial support from Burmah have enabled this book to be sold at a bargain price.

When I first thought of the idea, I didn't want the book to be just about the Premiership, but to contain all the elements that have helped make STFC what it is today. The present, after all, is only possible because of the past.

Just as Rikki has a vision for Burmah and STFC, I had a vision for what I wanted this book to be – a celebration. Thanks to Burmah the vision has become a reality.

Also thanks to John Gorman for giving me the time to interview him in full and get a glimpse of the man behind the moustache, Glenn Hoddle for his frank, honest interview, Lou Macari and Ossie Ardiles for theirs, Dave Hay for all his help and Swindon Town Chairman Ray Hardman for giving me full access to the Club, players and facilities.

Also Paul Plowman for his help with statistics as well as the loan of his pictures, and Andrea Elliot and Beverley Allbright at the Club for their assistance.

Thanks are also due to the players for their profiles and the behind-the-scenes staff for their matchday experiences.

Also to Robert for his endless patience, Nick Arkell for putting the wheels in motion and Peter Arkell for his continued support.

Special thanks to everyone at Burmah Petroleum Fuels, in particular Richard Miles, Marketing Director, Peter Atkinson, Manager, Marketing, Debbie Robinson, Sue Allen and Tracey Gatiss.

Last but certainly not least, thanks to Malcolm Jackson for the production and design and Keith Brain for his brilliant indexing and proof-reading skills.

Finally, thanks to you, the fans. Because without you there wouldn't have been a book. I know I've left someone out – apologies if I have.

....

Photographs courtesy of Keith Brain, Burmah Petroleum Fuels, Bristol United Press, Andy Crook, CBM, Calyx, Dave Evans (Wiltshire Newspapers), Steve Richards and Paul Plowman.

Historical information has been obtained from 'The Robins – a History of Swindon Town' by Dick Mattick.

Statistics courtesy of Paul Plowman.

Printed in Swindon, England.

Previous page *Paul Bodin scores from the penalty spot during the Wembley play-off final against Leicester City and puts the Town into the Premiership.*

CONTENTS

INTRODUCTION

WELCOME to 'Town at the Top' - a book which officially celebrates a landmark in the Club's history.

Our entry into the Carling Premiership - the finest soccer league in the world - and our first season against the top teams in the country have truly been remarkable achievements. Who would have thought that we would be entertaining the likes of Liverpool, Man. Utd. and Spurs regularly at the County Ground?

The fact that we have won many friends playing these famous teams is reason to celebrate by itself. It is also a fitting tribute to all the hard work, loyalty and dedication that has gone into the Club over the years.

Of course, none of this would have been possible without the tremendous support of you, the fans. No Club could ask for more.

This book pays tribute to the Town's rise to the top. It traces the path to the Premiership and charts the Club's development from humble beginnings.

The four managers who each played vital roles in the Club's rise tell their stories, including John Gorman who explains what Swindon means to him and why he turned down Glenn Hoddle's offer to follow him to Chelsea.

The players are profiled and pictured in action and there is a glimpse behind the scenes at those unsung heroes of the County Ground- from our laundry lady to the staff in the administration office.

There is also a chapter on our sponsors, Burmah Petroleum Fuels, whose generous financial support has enabled us to concentrate not only on bringing great football to the Premiership, but enabled this book to be published at the affordable price of £9.99.

No matter what happens this season, you the fans now have a book chronicling a very special time for the Club - the first time the Town played at the Top.

R V Hardman.

Ray Hardman
Chairman
April 1994

Ray Hardman has been Chairman of STFC since September 1991. He has lived in Swindon since 1975 and has always loved football. He was a Development Director with McLean Homes for 15 years from which he retired last year.

1 The Path to the Top

How Swindon Town
joined the top flight

SWINDON Town fans are used to the ups and downs of football. They have had more than their fair share of bitter blows and precious few sweet victories.

But the 1992/93 season at last brought the club the success it deserved - and buried the ghost of the cruel demotion of three years earlier when top flight football was won on the field but lost in the corridors of power.

However, the path to the top was not smooth - and the nerves of steel that the Town's fans have developed over the years were to be tested on more than one occasion.

The triumphant 1992/93 campaign started in style with the Town facing Sunderland - the club beaten in the 1990 Wembley play-off. The scoreline read the same - 1-0 to Swindon - the goal coming from player-manager Glenn Hoddle in classic style from 35 yards.

The result, the goal and Swindon's fluid style of play served as early warnings for other teams. Bristol Rovers, Cambridge and Oxford suffered the same fate as Sunderland - Cambridge, the arch exponents of the long-ball game, were soundly beaten 4-1. Only Wolves interrupted the unbeaten run with a 2-2 draw.

A 6-0 away win at Torquay in the first leg of the Coca-Cola Cup third round gave the Town's strikers valuable target practice but the run was to end with a 1-0 defeat at home at

Player-manager Glenn Hoddle, pictured with No 6 Shaun Taylor, got the 1992/93 season off to a stylish start with a classic goal.

8

the hands of Premier League side Oldham.

Back in the league, victories were secured against Grimsby, Watford, Notts County, West Ham and Barnsley although Swindon's feet were kept on the ground by defeats against Charlton, Portsmouth and Brentford.

By the time Swindon met Kevin Keegan's Newcastle at St James's Park, the Tyneside club had staked a firm claim to the top of the table.

But Swindon refused to be daunted by the side, putting on a stunning display of skill in a far-from-boring 0-0 draw which thrilled millions of Sunday afternoon TV viewers.

If Newcastle were dead certs for promotion, then Swindon were the class act of the First Division.

Victory at home against Southend kept Swindon in second place but draws at Bristol City and Peterborough and a 4-2 defeat at home to Derby County saw the Town slip back down to fourth place.

Another defeat by the same margin - this time at Leicester when Colin Calderwood was sent off - showed up Swindon's problems in defence. Only floodlight failure at the County Ground saved the Town from defeat against Tranmere who were 2-1 up when the lights went out.

Swindon took an early exit from the FA Cup - going down 3-0 against QPR at Loftus Road in the third round. In the League fortunes fluctuated. A 1-0 win at Oxford was followed by a 0-0 draw at home to Birmingham, 2-2 at home to Charlton and a 2-1 defeat at Grimsby.

A play-off place was beginning to look a possibility rather than a probability when three wins in succession - 1-0 against Wolves and Sunderland and 3-0 against Millwall - put Swindon back on track.

A 1-0 defeat at Cambridge proved to be a momentary lapse and three more wins followed - 2-0 at home to Tranmere, 1-0 at home to Portsmouth and 4-0 away to Watford. The nine points proved invaluable and took Swindon to third place.

Another point was taken from a 1-1 draw at Southend before Newcastle came to the County Ground looking to consolidate their commanding lead at the top of the table.

But after Swindon went 1-0 down shortly before half-time the 17,936 crowd - the biggest of the season - saw Paul Bodin convert a penalty to make the scores level and then Calderwood snatch the winning goal.

The victory was all the more sweet as David Kerslake had just been sold to Leeds by cash-strapped Town to bring in a much- needed £500,000.

Just as Swindon appeared to be on a roll again, a 0-0 draw at Luton was followed by a 2-1 defeat at Derby. Bristol City were beaten at home 2-1 but the one point gained from the 0-0 result at Brentford's

Paul Bodin. His penalty against Newcastle levelled the scores. The Town went on to get a vital 2-1 win.

Shaun Taylor flies in to head home Swindon's third goal at Wembley.

Griffin Park proved to be more valuable - considering Swindon's strike force of Steve White and Dave Mitchell were both sent off in the first half.

Three points from a 1-0 win over Peterborough at the County Ground were cancelled out by a 3-1 defeat at Tranmere. The likelihood of a play-off place rather than automatic promotion was now strong after a 1-0 home win over Luton.

Easter Monday saw Swindon travel to First Division strugglers Birmingham City who were determined for a result.

With half-an-hour left it looked like they had achieved it with a 4-1 scoreline. But never-say-die Swindon fought back, leaving the field with a 6-4 win, including a hat-trick from Mitchell, after a

Wembley here we come! l-r Craig Maskell, Nicky Summerbee and Paul Bodin celebrate getting to the play-off final.

remarkable turn around.

Two 1-1 draws with Leicester and Notts County kept the Town in the play-offs but the season's last two matches saw two defeats - 3-1 at home to West Ham and 1-0 away to Barnsley.

The West Ham result seemed to confirm the view at the Club that there was a jinx everytime TV cameras filmed a Swindon game. The side had not won while being broadcast - a jinx that had to be broken.

The first leg of the play-off semi-finals against Tranmere saw the Town take a commanding lead of 3-0 at half-time. Tranmere pulled one back to give Swindon a two-goal advantage to take North for the second leg.

The tense game ended with Tranmere winning 3-2 on the night but losing on aggregate to open the way for a Wembley play-off final between Swindon and Leicester.

Few of the 35,000 Swindon supporters who made the journey to Wembley would have predicted such a hugely enjoyable, but nail-biting, game.

The Town side that ran out onto the famous turf to huge cheers was; Digby, Summerbee, Bodin, Hoddle, Calderwood, Taylor, Moncur, MacLaren, Ling, Maskell (sub, White), Mitchell.

Just as he had scored the magnificent opening goal of the season, Glenn Hoddle paved the way for Swindon's success in the last game of the season.

The former England international drew on all his experience to take command of the game for Swindon. It was Hoddle who with a perfectly placed shot, opened the scoring for Swindon and sent the side in at half-time 1-0 up.

It's ours! Glenn Hoddle holds aloft the play-off final trophy at Wembley.

The dynamic duo. Gorman and Hoddle with the play-offs trophy.

Goals from Craig Maskell and Shaun Taylor gave Swindon a comfortable 3-0 lead and with half-an-hour to go it seemed the Town would cruise to victory.

But three goals in 11 minutes from Leicester saw the nerves of the Swindon supporters once again on edge.

Celebrations at Wembley after the thrilling seven-goal final.

With just six minutes to go Steve White, brought on for Maskell, was fouled by the Leicester keeper.

Paul Bodin, who had done much to get Swindon to Wembley, stepped up to take the kick as a strange hush descended on the vast stadium.

Many Swindon fans could not bear to watch - but Bodin tucked away the penalty to put the Town in the top flight of English soccer.

For a Club that had never played at the top in its 112-year history, a new chapter was about to begin.

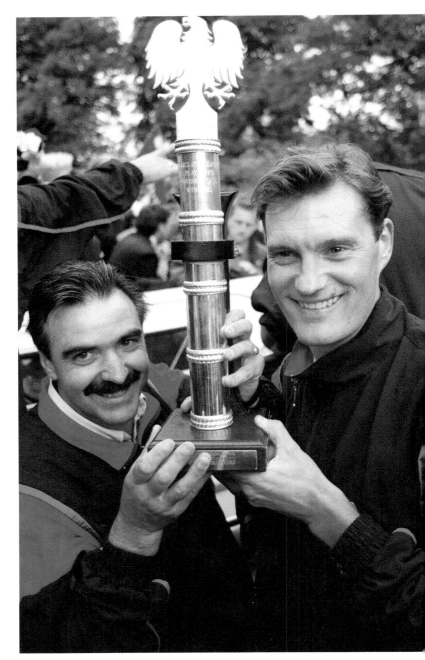

CONGRATULATIONS SWINDON TOWN
WE'RE UP WHERE WE BELONG

CHARTER

HAVE A NICE DAY

The bus-top victory celebrations start at the County Ground. Thousands of people lined the route around the streets of Swindon.

2 From Part-time to Big-time

A brief history of the Club

AN unremarkable 2-2 draw played between two local sides on a field is hardly the stuff that legends are made of. But it was such a match that saw the birth of Swindon Town Football Club.

And the unlikely figure who created the Club was one Reverend William Pitt. In true Victorian spirit the Rev Pitt organised soccer matches between local young men whose weekdays were spent toiling in Swindon's huge GWR railworks.

But the Rev could hardly have realised the significance when he invited St Mark's Young Men's Friendly Society to play The Spartans of Old Swindon on a field in Old Town on 12 November 1881.

At the end of the game the teams decided to merge to form one club for the town - to be known as The Swindon Football Club.

A club calling itself Swindon Association FC was already in existence. The Swindon Advertiser of 13 December 1879 has a report of a 4-0 defeat against Rover FC. In the Swindon Association side that day was a Rev Pitt although whether this team or the one formed in 1881 is the true foundation of Swindon Town is shrouded in mystery.

Len Skiller, the Town's pre-First World War goalkeeper. He was nicknamed The Cap after the headgear he wore in goal.

However, the humble beginnings of the Club are shown by the fact that it had difficulty finding a home ground - and even when it settled on playing at The Croft in Old Town the teams had to change in the Fountain pub.

The Club quickly found success on the field, winning the Wiltshire Senior Cup six years in succession. By 1894 it was invited to become a founder member of the Southern League along with teams like Millwall, Southampton and Luton, and two years later moved to the County Ground. The first stand was built at this time with a £300 loan from Arkell's Brewery.

The Club achieved little during its early years in the Southern League and it was not until 1907 that its fortunes turned. In that year the great Harold Fleming signed for the Town - and changed its history.

A teetotaller and strict Christian - he refused to play on Christmas Day and Good Friday - he became the first hero in a Swindon shirt.

With the inspirational Fleming playing inside-right, the pre-First World War Swindon team collected the Southern League championship in 1911 and a reputation as cup giant-killers, taking out top sides of the time like Manchester United, Manchester City, Everton and Tottenham.

Although Fleming, who was capped for England 12 times, has a special place in the history of Swindon Town - he is the only player to have a local road named after him - the Club

PROMINENT FOOTBALLERS.

L. SKILLER.
SWINDON TOWN.

The team that earned the reputation as cup giant-killers, with Harold Fleming second from right in front row.

he left in 1924 had changed little to the one he had joined 17 years earlier.

Many players were still part-timers and for the professionals, wages were low. The club, now in the Third Division (South), had little financial muscle and could not compete in the emerging transfer market.

But one shrewd signing was to pay dividends for the Club. For just £110 - even in 1926 a low sum - Swindon bought Harry Morris from Swansea.

Morris was to write his name in the Club's record books with his outstanding goal-scoring ability. In his second season for Swindon his goal tally was 47 - including five in one home game against QPR - a record that stands to this day.

With Morris in the side, Swindon regained its reputation for cup giant-killing, beating Manchester United at Old Trafford 2-0

in 1930 only to lose in the next round to Manchester City 10-1 at Maine Road.

One of Morris's contemporaries at this time was winger Bertie 'twinkletoes' Denyer who was also landlord of the Running Horse pub on Wootton Bassett Road. A war wound had left him with half his intestines missing and he had a rather unorthodox approach to training, describing it as "dropping into the ground on a Friday to do a bit of running and check if you were playing Saturday."

When £500 was raised for him at a benefit match he immediately pocketed it and went off to Margate for a holiday.

After a disastrous 1932/33 season when the Club had to apply for re-election to the League, Morris was sold to Clapton Orient. He had scored 217 goals for the Town.

Harry Morris. A player of legendary goal-scoring ability.

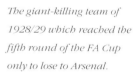

The giant-killing team of 1928/29 which reached the fifth round of the FA Cup only to lose to Arsenal.

Finances improved slightly with more cup runs and good gates including 23,000 for a midweek afternoon third round

Team line-up for the FA Cup tie at Brighton in 1934. Shirts were not numbered- but the referee appears to be no. 12.

Right The Swindon Town line-up for the 1947/48 season.

replay against Grimsby in 1938. But the size of the crowds concerned the local police - and the number of officers on duty at the County Ground was increased from four to seven.

The 1939/40 season kicked off with the opening of a new stand at the Town End - then called the Hotel End. A hundred season tickets were allocated at £3.3 shillings each for men and £2.2 shillings for ladies.

But only three games of the season were played before the War caused the League to be disbanded although games continued in regional leagues.

Ironically the Club's financial situation improved during the War. One of the stands was requisitioned as an air-raid shelter, the wages of players not serving in the armed forces were scrapped and replaced by appearance fees and sheep were allowed to graze on the pitch.

In the post-War years the Town achieved little apart

Fixture card for the 1939/40 season when only the first three games were played.

from a record defeat of 9-0 at Torquay, elimination from the FA Cup 4-1 at non-league Hastings and a record all-ticket crowd of 28,140 at the County Ground for a cup-tie with First Division Stoke City. Even with outstanding players like Welsh international Billy Lucas and the formidable Maurice Owen, the side floundered.

Poor performances made it look likely that the Club would find itself in the Fourth Division when the Third Divisions (North and South) merged in 1958. But it finished fourth and secured a place in the new Third Division.

A policy adopted in the 1950s when the Club's finances were stretched now began to pay-off under the managership of Bert Head. It had been decided, because of the spiralling cost of players on the transfer market, to nurture 'homegrown' talent. Young players showing ability were coached through youth leagues until they were ready to

join the first team.

By the 1960/61 season Ernie Hunt and Mike Summerbee

Roger Smart, right, *and Ernie Hunt*, below. *They became key players in the Town's revival in the Sixties.*

Rogers and the nucleus of the team that was to achieve Swindon's first major title at the end of the decade had been formed.

Even the big freeze of 1963 could not stop the young side. One of the few League games during that winter was one played at the County Ground against QPR.

On a snow-packed and sanded pitch with marking in blue and wearing basketball boots, Swindon ploughed into the Londoners, crushing them 5-0.

The basketball boots worked again at Luton in the Cup although First Division Everton ended Swindon's Wembley dream in the following round, winning 5-1 at the County Ground.

The young side was now free to concentrate on promotion. A run of good results made it a possibility and it all hinged on two points from the last home game of the season against Shrewsbury.

The scores were level at 0-0 until one minute from the final whistle when Roger Smart gave the crowd the goal they wanted and brought Second Division soccer to the County Ground for the first time.

The 1963/64 season had a fairytale start for Swindon. The young side found itself top of the Division and possible promotion contenders, only to see the tide turn in mid-season with a flurry of poor results.

The season ended with the Town in the reasonable position of 14th. The team had also had a run in the cup to the fifth round when West Ham put them out 3-1 at the County Ground in front of a new record crowd of 28,582.

The nurturing of young talent had continued despite the

had come through this system. They joined a side so young it became nicknamed Bert's Babes.

But what the players lacked in League experience they made up for in enthusiasm and skill. By the 1962/63 season Summerbee and Hunt had been joined by Roger Smart and Don

17

Burmah

youth of the first team and Swindon reached the final of the FA Youth Trophy for the first time in its history - losing to a Manchester United side that included a young George Best.

The following season saw Swindon's fate sealed again by the last game - although this time a defeat at Southampton meant relegation back to the Third Division. Ernie Hunt had been injured for much of the season.

The 1965/66 campaign started without Bert Head, who had been sacked after relegation, and with Mike Summerbee and Ernie Hunt both transfer-listed due to financial pressures.

Summerbee went to Manchester City and Hunt to Wolves but disgruntled fans were soothed by a spate of high-scoring victories. Don Rogers got two hat-tricks in 6-0 and 5-0 wins over York City and Reading respectively, while Keith East got four against Merthyr Tydfil in the Cup and equalled Harry Morris's record of five against Mansfield.

The following season saw a return to Swindon's giant-killing days in the Cup. The Town's name came out of the bag with West Ham's in the third round.

The Hammers' side boasted three of England's World Cup heroes - Hurst, Moore and Peters - but they found their match in Swindon's young talent. After a 3-3 draw at Upton Park, West Ham were despatched 3-1 in the replay at the County Ground.

Mike Summerbee. He was transferred because of the Club's cash problems.

Bert Head. Sacked after the Town's relegation back to the Third Division.

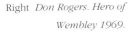

Right Don Rogers. Hero of Wembley 1969.

Swindon lasted until the fifth round when the tie with Nottingham Forest went to three games before the Midlands side secured victory.

The Town's exploits in the Cup were not repeated in the League and mid-table positions became routine. But it was to be in another cup - the League Cup - that Swindon achieved its greatest victory in its history to that date.

The League Cup campaign took in victories over Torquay, Bradford City, Blackburn and Coventry. The quarter-final against Derby went to a replay before being decided but it was at the semi-final stage that Swindon fans needed nerves of steel.

It was played over two legs against Burnley - then a side to be reckoned with. Swindon won the first leg away 2-1 only to lose at home by the same margin, making the two teams equal on aggregate.

In the replay Swindon held a one goal lead until the 90th minute when Burnley equalised. When the Lancashire club scored in the first minute of extra time it seemed Swindon's Wembley dream would be over for another season. But an own goal and one from Peter Noble booked Swindon's tickets to the Final.

The team that ran out onto the hallowed, but muddy, turf of Wembley on 15 March 1969 to face the mighty Arsenal may have been wearing its change-strip of all white, but the line-up was familiar to the thousands of Swindon fans who had travelled to London that day.

Peter Downsborough, Rod Thomas, John Trollope, Joe Butler, Frank Burrows, Stan Harland, Don Heath, Roger Smart, John Smith, Peter Noble and Don Rogers with Willie Penman on the bench were clearly the under-dogs against an Arsenal side

Don Rogers makes sure that the Football League Cup comes to Swindon by scoring his second goal of the match and the third for Town. Wembley Football League Cup Final, 15th March, 1969
This photograph is published by courtesy of Wiltshire Newspapers.

that included Bobby Gould, George Armstrong and Bob Wilson.

And when at the end of ordinary time the scores were level at 1-1 (Smart had scored after 35 minutes but Gould got the equaliser six minutes before time) all the signs were that the experience of Arsenal would see them lift the cup.

But it was Don Rogers who was to serve up a fairytale ending and give Swindon their first major honour. As the Wembley pitch turned into a mud bath, Rogers' agility came to the fore. His two

goals - one in each half of extra time - dealt Arsenal the killer blow and it was Harland who held the League Cup aloft to roars from the crowd that afternoon.

Swindon's dogged determination at Wembley was to pay-off in the League, too.

They finished second to Watford - being pipped to the championship medals only by a poorer goal average.

Back in Division Two the Town mounted an immediate promotion challenge, finishing a well-deserved fifth and reached round six of

John Trollope. Despite his youth he was a key player in Swindon sides throughout the Sixties.

Far Left *Fairytale ending. Don Rogers scores his second and Swindon's third goal to win the League Cup.*

"HERE IT IS, SUPPORTERS, WE'VE WON IT".
This photograph is published by courtesy of The Daily Express

Wembley wonders. Swindon, very much the underdogs, with the League Cup.

the FA Cup, losing to Leeds 2-0 - a result which flattered the famous side. The season ended with Swindon travelling to Naples

Swindon's Italian job. A brief taste of European soccer.

to win the Anglo-Italian Cup 3-0. It was the Town's second title in European football that season, the first being the Anglo-Italian Cup Winners' Cup which was collected with a 5-2 aggregate win over AS Roma.

Danny Williams, the manager who had taken Swindon to Wembley for the first time in its history, left the Club to be replaced by Dave Mackay who had just taken Derby County into the First Division.

Instead of repeating this feat at Swindon, Mackay's short term was a near-disaster for the Club. Despite playing at the highest level of its history, gates were falling, finances were stretched and pressure to sell players grew.

Mackay sold Don Rogers for £147,000 to Crystal Palace - then left Swindon for 'personal reasons'. Within days he was appointed manager at Nottingham Forest - a fact that angered Town fans no end.

That the Club should slip back into the Third Division surprised no-one. Gates continued to fall and more players were sold in the vicious circle of lower division football. Danny Williams returned as manager and made a popular move by bringing Don Rogers back to the County Ground - a move so popular the crowd at his first home match doubled to 10,000.

But the Town needed more than a touch of the Rogers'

magic. The mid and late 1970s saw the Club rooted firmly in Division Three. The only bright spot was a good run in the League Cup which ended with defeat against Wolves in the semi-finals, in February 1980.

Frank Burrows and Bobby Smith came and went as managers but it was John Trollope, who played 832 times for the Club, who was the unluckiest in the dugout. Having escaped relegation to the Fourth Divison in the 1980/81 season in the last game of the term the inevitable happened the following season.

A run of poor results in the Town's first term in Divison Four saw Trollope relieved of his duties. New manager Ken Beamish faired little better, having to break his promise not to sell Paul Rideout, whose transfer to Villa for £175,000 at least eased the financial plight of the Club.

Swindon finished the 1983/84 season 17th in the table and the Club was at its lowest ebb. What it needed was a miracle - and in former Manchester United and Scottish international Lou Macari it found one.

Things were not easy for Macari at first. The Club limped out of the FA Cup with an embarrassing defeat at the hands of non-league Dagenham. A misunderstanding with the board saw Macari dismissed - only for the decision to be overturned five days later.

Macari brought a new discipline to the team, which he strengthened when he could bearing in mind the difficult state of the Club's finances. He brought in a handful of skilled players including Colin Calderwood and Steve White and lifted the spirits of the Club.

On the up. Swindon players
celebrate their play-off victory
at Selhurst Park.

Halfway through the 1985/86 season the Town reached the top of the Fourth Division - and stayed there for the rest of the season.

Macari could do no wrong. A year after getting into the Third Division Swindon were leaving it again - this time for the Second after victories in the play-offs against Wigan and Gillingham which went to a third match before a decisive result.

The 1987/88 season saw the Town finish a creditable halfway in the Second Division. But there was no stopping Macari's side and at the end of the 1988/89 campaign they were knocking on the door of football's top flight for the first time in the Club's history.

The Town were no match for Crystal Palace in the play-offs - but it seemed only a matter of time before Swindon got into the First Division.

That was not to be under Macari's stewardship, though. He

left the Club after the Palace play-off to move first to West Ham, then Birmingham, Stoke and Celtic.

The manager who brought First Division football to the County Ground for the first time was another player who had trod the international stage and played in England's top flight. Like Macari, Ossie Ardiles had no managerial experience when he came to Swindon - but what he lacked in the office side of the game he made up for on the pitch.

With roughly the same squad as his predecessor he brought an entirely different style of play to the County Ground. In sharp contrast to Macari's long-ball game, Ardiles introduced a fluent form of play which won Swindon widespread admiration.

It was no surprise that Swindon got into the promotion play-offs at the end of the season. Having taken-out Blackburn over two legs, Swindon faced Sunderland at Wembley in the play-off final.

Thousands of Swindon fans made the journey to London to see Sunderland defeated by the only goal of the game.

Swindon had made it into the big-time for the first time in its history. But the celebrations were to be cut short in the cruellest way.

An investigation of the Club's finances was already taking place when the side travelled to Wembley. The then-Chairman Gary Herbert had offered to withdraw the Club from the play-offs if no action was taken - but the Football League case was postponed.

When the blow was dealt it was a devastating one. The League Commission demoted Swindon to the Third Division for its misdemeanours, which involved paying players extra untaxed amounts.

The decision caused uproar in Swindon. There were peti-

Physio Kevin Morris salutes promotion to the First Division at the Wembley play-off final against Sunderland. But the celebrations were short-lived.

The Swindon squad 1993/94 season with directors and County Ground staff.

tions, a march and rally, threats of legal action by individual fans who felt cheated, and questions in the House of Commons by MP Simon Coombs.

The fans realised the Club had been made an example of. They wanted the guilty to be punished, not the loyal supporters who had followed the Club from the depths of the Fourth Division.

Some justice was done when the Club's appeal to the FA resulted in Swindon being put back into the Second Division - but the whole episode left a bitter after-taste in Swindon.

Ardiles stayed for part of the 1991/92 season but the temptation of more money for players took him Newcastle. His replacement was again a tremendously gifted international player taking his first step into management.

Glenn Hoddle continued, and improved on, Ardiles' style of play but the Town struggled and narrowly avoided relegation. The following season the Club faired better on the field but financial pressures again meant key players had to be sold.

The side finished eighth - a creditable position and one from which it could spring its promotion challenge, gain - and hopefully, retain - a place at the top of English soccer and bury the ghosts of the illegal payments scandal three years before.

◆◆◆◆◆◆

3 Players in Profile

The main squad in words and pictures

FRASER DIGBY

Position: Goalkeeper

Squad No: 1

Date of Birth: 23.4.67

Place of Birth: Sheffield

Height: 6ft 2ins

Weight: 13st 4lbs

Career details

Manchester Utd

Number of appearances for STFC: 345

Favourite food: Any pasta dishes

Favourite pop group/singer: M People

Favourite TV prog: Absolutely Fabulous

Favourite Film: A Few Good Men

Most admired footballer: Ray Clemence

Signature:

Information accurate at time of publication 19.2.94

NICKY SUMMERBEE

Position: Defender

Squad No: 2

Date of Birth: 26.8.71

Place of Birth: Altrincham

Height: 5ft 8ins

Weight: 11st 8lbs

Career details

Number of appearances for STFC: 117 and goals 6

Favourite food: Steak

Favourite pop group/singer: Lisa Stansfield

Favourite TV prog: Only Fools and Horses

Favourite Film: A Few Good Men

Most admired footballer: Norman Whiteside

Signature:

PAUL BODIN

Position: Left back/midfield

Squad No: 3

Date of Birth: 13.9.64

Place of Birth: Cardiff

Height: 6ft

Weight: 12st 2lbs

Career details

Newport County 61 appearances 1 goal

Cardiff City 75 appearances 4 goals

Bath City 106 appearances 32 goals

Crystal Palace 9 appearances

Plus 20 Wales caps

Number of appearances for STFC: 149 and goals 22

Favourite food: Steak, pasta

Favourite pop group/singer: Genesis

Favourite TV prog: Brookside

Favourite Film: Ghost

Most admired footballers: Glenn Hoddle and George Best

Signature:

LUC NIJHOLT

Position: Midfield/defender

Squad No: 5

Date of Birth: 29.7.61

Place of Birth: Zaandam

Height: 5ft 11ins

Weight: 12st 4lbs

Career details

Haarlem 210 appearances 20 goals

AZ69 Alkmaar 20 appearances 1 goal

Utrecht 22 appearances 3 goals

Aldboys Basel 34 appearances 7 goals

Motherwell 100 appearances 7 goals

Number of appearances for STFC: 20

Favourite food: Italian

Favourite pop group/singer: M People

Favourite TV prog: Mr Bean and Spitting Image

Favourite Film: Once Upon a time in America

Most admired footballer: Johan Neeskens

Signature:

SHAUN TAYLOR

Position: Centre half

Squad No: 6

Date of Birth: 26.2.62

Place of birth: Plymouth

Height: 6ft 1in

Weight: 12st 7lbs

Career details

Exeter City 200 league and 15 cup appearances 12 goals

Number of appearances for STFC: 143 and goals 20

Favourite food: Pasta

Favourite pop group/singer: Phil Collins

Favourite TV prog: Question of Sport

Favourite Film: Dances with Wolves

Most admired footballer: Bryan Robson

Signature:

JOHN MONCUR

Position: Midfield

Squad No: 7

Date of Birth: 22.9.66

Place of Birth: Stepney (London)

Height: 5ft 9ins

Weight: 11st

Career details

Tottenham 21 appearances

Plus loans spells with Doncaster
Rovers, Cambridge Utd,
Portsmouth, Brentford, Ipswich and
Notts Forest

Number of appearances for STFC: 56 and
goals 4

Favourite food: Hamburgers

Favourite pop group/singer: Boyz II Men

Favourite TV prog: Minder

Favourite Film: Scarface

Most admired footballer: Gazza

Signature:

ROSS MACLAREN

Position: Midfield

Squad No: 8

Date of Birth: 14.4.62

Place of Birth: Edinburgh

Height: 5ft 10ins

Weight: 13st 13lbs

Career details

Shrewsbury 161 appearances 18 goals

Derby 122 appearances 4 goals

Number of appearances for STFC: 246 and
goals 12

Favourite food: Chinese

Favourite pop group/singer: Phil
Collins

Favourite TV prog: Sport

Favourite Film: The Long Good Friday

Most admired footballer: George Best

Signature:

JAN AAGE FJORTOFT

Position: Forward

Squad No: 9

Date of Birth: 10.1.67

Place of Birth: Aalesund, Norway

Height: 6ft 3ins

Weight: 13st 6lbs

Career details

Hodd (Norway) 22 appearances 25 goals

Ham-Kam 44 appearances 18 goals

Lillestrom 33 appearances 20 goals

Rapid Vienna 125 appearances 75 goals

Number of appearances for STFC: 16 and goals 7

Favourite food: Pasta

Favourite pop group/singer: The Beatles

Favourite TV prog: Sport and News

Favourite Film: One Flew Over The Cuckoo's Nest

Most admired footballer: Johan Cruyff

Signature:

MARTIN LING

Position: Midfield

Squad No: 10

Date of Birth: 15.7.66

Place of birth: London

Height: 5ft 8ins

Weight: 10st 4lbs

Career details

Exeter City 134 appearances 14 goals

Mansfield Town (loan) 4 appearances

Southend United 175 appearances 36 goals

Number of appearances for STFC: 71 and goals 1

Favourite food: Italian (pasta)

Favourite pop group/singer: Genesis

Favourite TV prog: Cheers

Favourite Film: Fatal Attraction

Most admired footballer: Paul Gascoigne

Signature:

STEVE WHITE

Position: Centre forward
Squad No: 12
Date of Birth: 2.1.59
Place of Birth: Chipping Sodbury
Height: 5ft 11ins
Weight: 12 stone
Career details
Bristol Rovers 50 appearances 20 goals
Luton Town 76 appearances 25 goals
Charlton Athletic 29 appearances 12 goals
Bristol Rovers 101 appearances 24 goals
Number of appearances for STFC: 230 and goals 111
Favourite food: Steak and chips
Favourite pop group/singer: Michael Jackson
Favourite TV prog: Only Fools and Horses
Favourite Film: Any Clint Eastwood film
Most admired footballer Kevin Keegan

Signature:

ADRIAN WHITBREAD

Position: Defender
Squad No: 14
Date of Birth: 22.10.71
Place of birth: Epping, Essex
Height: 6ft 1in
Weight: 13st
Career details
Leyton Orient 180 appearances 3 goals
Number of appearances for STFC: 28 and goals 1
Favourite food: Chinese or steak
Favourite pop group/singer: Take That
Favourite TV prog: Only Fools and Horses
Favourite Film: A Few Good Men
Most admired footballer: Andy Mutch

Signature:

KEVIN HORLOCK

Position: Left back

Squad No: 16

Date of Birth: 1.11.72

Place of Birth: Erith, Kent

Height: 5ft 11ins

Weight: 12 stone

Career details

Number of appearances for STFC: 44 and goals 1

Favourite food: Fry up

Favourite pop group/singer: Simply Red

Favourite TV prog: Brookside

Favourite Film: The Godfather

Most admired footballer: None

Signature:

NICKY HAMMOND

Position: Goalkeeper

Squad No: 23

Date of Birth: 7.9.67.

Place of Birth: Hornchurch (Essex)

Height: 6ft

Weight: 12st 10lbs

Career details

Apprentice and young professional at Arsenal (no appearances)

On loan to Bristol Rovers, Aberdeen and Peterborough

Number of appearances for STFC: 82

Favourite food: Chinese

Favourite pop group/singer: Likes most kinds of music.

Favourite TV prog: Documentaries

Favourite Film: The Graduate

Most admired footballer: David Seaman

Signature:

ANDY MUTCH

Position: Forward

Squad No: 25

Date of Birth: 28.12.63

Place of Birth: Liverpool

Height: 5ft 10ins

Weight: 12st

Career details

Wolves 297 appearances 97 goals

Number of appearances for STFC: 31 and goals 9

Favourite food: Pasta

Favourite pop group/singer: Don Henly and Prince

Favourite TV prog: Crimewatch

Favourite Film: Patriot Games

Most admired footballer: Kenny Dalglish

Signature:

TERRY FENWICK

Position: Defender

Squad No: 26

Date of Birth: 17.11.59

Place of Birth: Sunderland

Height: 5ft 10ins

Weight: 12st

Career details

Crystal Palace 70 appearances

QPR 550 appearances 33 goals

Spurs 93 appearances and 53 goals

Plus 20 England caps

Number of appearances for STFC: 23

Favourite food: English roast

Favourite pop group/singer: Rolling Stones

Favourite TV prog: Only Fools and Horses

Favourite Film: The Godfather

Most admired footballer: Terry Venables

Signature:

KEITH SCOTT

Position: Centre forward

Squad No: 27

Date of Birth: 9.6.67

Place of Birth: Westminster (London)

Height: 6ft 3ins

Weight: 14st

Career details

Lincoln City 11 appearances 2 goals

Wycombe Wanderers 135 appearances 75 goals

Number of appearances for STFC: 14 and goals 4

Favourite food: Pasta

Favourite pop group/singer: Police

Favourite TV prog: Coronation St

Favourite Film: All spaghetti westerns

Most admired footballer: "All forwards who score on a regular basis and have a good goals to games ratio."

Signature:

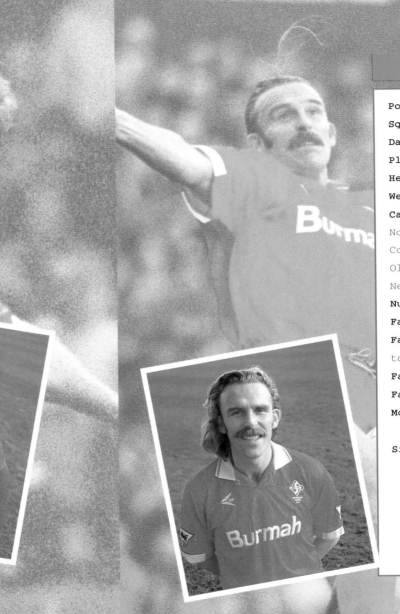

BRIAN KILCLINE

Position: Centre back

Squad No: 31

Date of Birth: 7.5.62

Place of birth: Nottingham

Height: 6ft 4ins

Weight: 14st 10lbs

Career details

Notts County 158 appearances 9 goals

Coventry City 173 appearances 28 goals

Oldham Athletic 8 appearances

Newcastle 31 appearamces

Number of appearances for STFC: 4

Favourite food: Anything

Favourite pop group/singer: Too many to mention

Favourite TV prog: Soldier Soldier

Favourite Film: Midnight Express

Most admired footballer: George Best

Signature:

Part of the community. Jonathan Trigg, left, and Terry O'Connor at a children's Christmas party at Swindon's Princess Margaret Hospital.

SWINDON TOWN IN THE COMMUNITY

SWINDON Town takes its role in the local community very seriously. Not only is it important to local people but in turn, the community is important to the Club.

Two years ago it was decided to set up a department at the County Ground to strengthen the links between the Club and the community.

The scheme has been a huge success involving thousands of people not just from Swindon but nearby towns including Newbury and Melksham.

Former Sunderland professional Jonathan Trigg, 22, runs the scheme with ex-Bristol City player Terry Connor. Swindon is one of the few clubs in the country to have two community officers - a sign of how seriously the Club takes the scheme.

Terry, 31, joined last September through a sponsorship deal with Kevin Jackson Windows of Melksham.

"It's wonderful that everyone has taken the scheme to their hearts," said Jonathan.

Burmah

The scheme gets all sections of the community involved from children as young as six to the elderly. Youth clubs, groups for disabled people and the probation service are also involved.

The scheme has proved so popular with its coaching courses for schools and summer training events that there is a waiting list.

As well as going into schools and supervising coaching sessions, youngsters visit the County Ground for a behind-the-scenes tour.

"It's wonderful to see the looks on their faces when they look at the dressing rooms then run out of the tunnel onto the pitch. It makes it all worthwhile," said Jonathan.

Jonathan and Terry run summer courses in Swindon and the surrounding towns for six to sixteen year-olds which have proved very popular for would-be soccer stars.

The pair visit hospitals and old peoples' Clubs.

"Football is for everyone - young and old!" added Jonathan.

Terry and Jonathan at the County Ground.

Far Right *Andy Rowland.*

THE RESERVES

ANDY Rowland has been the Reserve Team manager since 1986.

He started his professional football career as an apprentice with Bury. Two years later he got into the first team.

His first game with Bury's main team was with Swindon Town!

In 1978 he joined Swindon as a player when he was sold by Bury by manager Bob Smith for £90,000.

He worked his way into coaching. In 1986, he became reserve team manager and also played with the reserve team.

His responsibility is to look after the reserves and shape them into first team players.

The responsibilties of a reserve player are different from those in the youth team, according to Andy, and he must prepare them for the change - mentally and physically.

"They are no longer with lads their own age, size or strength and must adapt - ready for when they play with the main squad."

Andy rarely gets to see Swindon play, because most of his time is spent scouting.

ADRIAN VIVEASH

ANDREW THOMSON

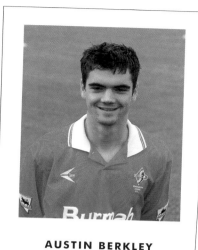

AUSTIN BERKLEY

CHRIS HAMON

MARCUS PHILLIPS

WAYNE O'SULLIVAN

EDWIN MURRAY

LEE MIDDLETON

* Also in the Reserves, Ty Gooden (not pictured).

Although the Club's chief scout is Les O'Neill, Andy still regularly goes scouting. He has regular contact with John Trollope of Swindon Youths.

"It's wonderful to look out for Swindon's future talent. There is a certain magic and excitement watching other teams and spotting a player with that certain something," said Andy.

4 Count-down to Kick-Off

Behind the scenes at the County Ground

WHEN the referee blows his whistle at 3pm to start the game all eyes are on the pitch. But long before the teams and the fans arrive, the County Ground is a hive of activity.

Behind-the-scenes the unsung heroes of Swindon Town have been busy for hours to make sure the 90 minutes of football go smoothly.

Activity at the County Ground on match day starts at 6.30am - seven-and-a-half hours before kick-off.

Bob Richins and Pete Smith arrive to start cleaning the hospitality suites. They have been volunteers since 1969 but are now on the payroll. They clean all the suites from top to bottom including the polishing and vacuuming and even clean the toilets!

They are joined at around 8am by two chefs from Applewood Catering who start preparing the 340 meals that will be eaten in the suites. An hour later the 20 waiters, waitresses and washers-up arrive to make their preparations.

Checking everything they do is Jackie Stewart of Applewood. Jackie formed the company specially to serve the food at Swindon Town. The company has no other clients and Jackie doesn't want any!

She became a Town fan after going to Wembley for the play-off final against Leicester. Her husband Alex, then the manager of Swindon's De Vere hotel, organised the post-match party at the hotel. Before that, she wasn't remotely interested in football.

"When we are working, it gives us all such a high when we hear the roar of the crowd when the Town have scored a goal," said Jackie, who enjoys her work so much she doesn't mind missing the match.

Around the same time the Robins Club Shop opens - even six hours before kick-off there are keen fans who want souvenirs. Manager Paul Plowman works with assistant Natasha Coleman and volunteers Ann Alder, Marie Baxter and Becky Vaughn.

Paul, 44, has been a fan of the Town for 30 years. He started as a volunteer himself, helping in the shop on match days.

Last year he took redundancy from British Rail and became the Robins Club shop manager - an ideal job for him because of his love for the Club. He attends every game - home and away - and has a huge collection of old photos of Town players and programmes dating back to the 1920s bought mainly from fairs and private auctions.

Bob Richins, left, and Pete Smith brew up.

He also has an encyclopaedic knowledge of everything linked to Swindon Town, keeps files on every player and supplies match statistics to the Evening Advertiser. If Paul doesn't know it, it's not worth knowing.

The shop stocks everything the loyal fan can possibly want - from tracksuits and replica kits to pens and notepads. The shop had an immediate hit in February when it sold baseball caps with fake ponytails - so short-haired fans could look like Town defender and recent signing, Brian Kilcline.

The shop's busiest times are around noon and at half-time.

Anne, Becky and Marie are all mad-keen Town fans who like helping the Club. Anne, a Town supporter for 12 years, started out by making rolls to sell on coaches for away matches. Becky started working as a volunteer seven years ago when she got to know Anne and Paul, while Marie has worked in the shop for one season after being a programme seller.

All enjoy being involved in the Club. "It's so exciting to be a part of it!" said Marie.

The ticket office also opens at 9am but Tony Walker has often been processing tickets all night. He is backed by the rest of the ticket office team - Bernie Davies, Gary Derby and John Blackwell, the cashier

The ticket office is always busy with advance bookings for future matches and sorting out any spare tickets for that day's game.

An hour later, the programme sellers arrive. Paul Plowman supervises the 25 volunteers - including his mum Elizabeth who at 62, is the oldest. They get ready and go to to their various points around the ground where they stay until five minutes before kick-off when they are allowed in to watch the game free - the reward for their hard work.

Mum and son team: Elizabeth and Paul Plowman.

Just the ticket: Gary Derby, left, and Tony Walker in the office.

Burmah

Elizabeth said: "We both love the Club and do this work out of love more than anything else."

By 11.30am Bob and Pete have finished their cleaning and are joined by Barry Crewe and Stan Fryer who are in charge of maintenance. The four work under stadium manager Mike Hughes.

But Bob and Pete haven't finished their job for the day - and it is what they do next that gives them the greatest pleasure.

After checking their cleaning they change into their best clothes for their second role of the day - as tea 'ladies'.

They serve tea to the players an hour before the match and also at half-time. They have done this job for years and says Bob, it's worth doing the cleaning just for the honour of serving the players. They know exactly how each player likes his tea.

"It's still a thrill - even though we've been doing it for 25 years," they say in unison.

Should anything need repairing such as a toilet seat or even a seat in the stands, Stan and Barry are on hand. Even during the game they are there to tend to any repairs or emergency - standing at different ends of the stadium with mobile phones at the ready.

As well as being responsible for maintenance, Mike Hughes also has to oversee security and safety on match days.

Before each game a number of safety and security checks are carried out - all designed to minimise disruption to supporters but to maximise their safety and security.

Tasks such as checking the PA system, fire extinguishers, lighting and turnstiles are carried out and only when Mike is satisfied there are no problems can supporters be let into the ground.

Mike has been with the Town for ten years starting as the maintenance man. He worked on his own then but now he's in charge of his own maintenance team - Barry and Stan. Three years ago, he was appointed stadium manager and safety officer.

Fans queue for the matchday programme.

Police briefing. Supt. Glen Symes, left, and Chief Insp. Martyn Meeks discuss security and safety procedures with stadium manager Mike Hughes.

"Every day is different," he says. "That's what makes it exciting - and also the football!"

The 162 stewards, car park attendants and turnstile operators for the games are supplied by Recruit Agency.

Recruit manager Paul Penman has been at the ground since early morning and has already had a meeting with Mike Hughes and Club Secretary Jon Pollard.

The Taylor Report lays down strict guidelines on procedures to be followed at all football grounds. Links between the stewards and the police are vital and Recruit even has a controller sitting in the police box to act as a link.

At 12.30pm Paul issues the stewards with their yellow or orange (for fire marshalls) jackets. They are then briefed by Ray Rogers, the head steward and then by the police-commander Glen Symes.

This briefing covers general safety procedures, including how to deal with that day's away supporters and a general discussion about any recent incidents.

Mike Hughes is also at the briefing in his role as safety officer.

He sees briefings as a vital part of keeping the County Ground safe and secure. "They are important even though many of the stewards already know the drill, because there are always new people starting."

The stewards in the car park have been on patrol since 9am but the rush starts around 12.30pm.

The ambulances and nursing staff arrive at noon. There are usually three nurses and two doctors at the Club on match day to deal with any incidents either on or off the pitch - from stitches to resuscitation.

Meanwhile Geoff Warren, the Club's groundsman, arrives and gives the pitch the final once over. He also checks the lines and goals - nets and woodwork - for any last minute adjustments or repairs.

Geoff plays a key role for he is the person responsible for the most important piece of equipment the Club has - its pitch.

The work on the pitch really began soon after the last home match. Geoff makes any repairs to the pitch straight after a game and then three days before a match he starts to top-dress it - a job he does twice a week all through the season.

Geoff has been a groundsman in football for 20 years and

Pre-match briefing for stewards.

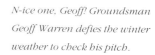

N-ice one, Geoff! Groundsman Geoff Warren defies the winter weather to check his pitch.

The control room: the nerve centre of the County Ground's security system.

a professional gardener for forty - starting his career as an apprentice groundsman with Birmingham Parks Department at the age of fifteen.

What he doesn't know about soil drainage and osmosis isn't worth knowing. After spells with Birmingham City and Bristol City football clubs, he went to work for Woodspring Council in Weston-Super-Mare where he lives.

He was head-hunted by Swindon Town in 1985 and then began a six-year labour of love to restore the pitch to its former glory.

"It was waterlogged and difficult to play on and the Club was losing games. The answer was so simple - there was no drainage," says Geoff.

He is there every match day to ensure the pitch is immaculate for the players. But he admits it's painful for him to watch what they do to it during a game.

And he admits for someone who puts so much tender loving care into the grass, his own garden would be a mess if his wife didn't look after it.

At 12.45pm Wally Cuss sets up the closed circuit TV system in the control room - a job he has done on-and-off for eight years first as a police officer, then after he retired last year, working for the Club.

Under the Taylor Report, clubs are responsible for their own security cameras.

The County Ground has six cameras at vantage points around the ground as well as a mobile camera operated by PC Chris Wilkins. Every monitor is taped and kept for at least a year.

Half-an-hour before kick-off Wally is joined by Supt. Glen Symes who oversees the entire police operation for each match.

The police have been around since 10am but half-an-hour

before kick-off, Supt. Symes goes up to the control room where he stays for the rest of the match. He is in contact with all the supervisors and officers by mobile phone.

The number of officers at each game depends on the threat of trouble. There can be as many as 100 constables and 22 supervisors at a match depending on which category it is in. Matches are graded A, B and C according to the risk. C is the highest risk and the police staff increased accordingly.

Supt. Symes has been commander in charge of operations for four years and deputy commander for six years before that, so is familiar with the routine.

Before arriving at the ground he will have discussed security measures at an 11.30am briefing with his supervisors at Swindon central police station. He will also have been in contact with police intelligence officers from all the clubs at the beginning of the season and again a fortnight before each game, when they update him on any recent trouble at the Clubs in their areas. He, in turn, updates them.

The number of police on duty at the ground is lower than a few years ago thanks to improved security and the good behaviour of Swindon fans.

"The crowd is anxious not to have trouble and enjoy the match, so any potential troublemaker is often dealt with by the public as well as the police. I look forward to the time when matches will be police-free. With the help of cameras and video that will soon become a reality," he said.

At 1pm Eddie Buckley, the Kit Manager, arrives. Eddie, 69, has been linked with the Club for more than 30 years.

He moved to Swindon from London in 1962 and started work as a machine operator with a local company. As it was night work, Eddie's days were free. He heard the Club wanted volunteers to help out and offered his services - first as a trainer with the youth team, then the Reserves.

In 1992, Eddie was put on the payroll as Kit Manager and is now responsible for the kits of all players - from main squad to the youth and reserve teams.

His first task on arriving at the ground is to have a meeting with John Gorman who gives him a list of who's playing. He does a final run-through of the kit, making sure the right kit is with the right player.

He also checks the boots have been cleaned properly by the

All kitted out: Kit Manager Eddie Buckley checks the strip.

41

apprentices and the correct types of stud or rubbers inserted. This is down to the player's personal preference and the pitch's condition.

Every apprentice is allocated one player's boots and makes sure they are cleaned properly.

Eddie is given all the clean kits the previous day by the laundry lady Jean Crewe, Barry's wife. She has been doing the job for almost four years.

"Barry did the laundry for a while, but he couldn't get his kits as clean as me!" Jean jokes. "He even let the colours run once!"

Wash-day Reds: laundry lady Jean Crewe's goal is the perfect wash!

JEAN'S TIP FOR A MUD-FREE WASH

Put your clothes in the washing machine in layers with Biotex between each layer. If it can get the mud out of players' kits, it can do anything; Jean swears by it!

WATCH THE HOME TEAM

semitron
circuit protection technology

she laughs.

Jean has always been a fan of the Town, watching every home match from Stratton Bank. Now, when the players run out on the pitch she is one of the proudest people in the crowd. She boasts that her reds are the reddest in the Premiership.

Most days she can be found in the laundry room with her 15 year-old industrial washing machine getting the kits brilliantly clean.

> *Jean gave Nicky Hammond a lucky horseshoe when he first arrived at the Club and was staying at the hostel. He's been carrying it in his kitbag ever since.*

"I love that machine and wouldn't use anything else!" she says.

She washes all the kits from main squad, youth and reserve teams and the under-14s. She washes all day long - proudly transforming the mud-caked shirts, shorts and socks into gleaming kits.

Her biggest enemy is mud and she cringes on a matchday when she sees players sliding around.

"I'm really pleased when Nicky Hammond saves a goal," says Jean. "But then I think, 'Oh no I've got to treat that one.' I wish he could save the goals without diving to the ground."

But Jean always gets the mud out - her secret is a pre-soak with Biotex.

Jean doesn't only wash kits. She is the Club's expert on stains. There isn't a stain that has defeated her! Word has soon got round and she treated the Chairman's blazer for a coffee stain once, that he couldn't get out. A bit of Biotex soon put paid to it.

"Ray Hardman came to me and said: 'Jean, if you can't get this out, no-one can!' "

She also helped out Luc Nijholt with his washing when he and his wife moved to Swindon with their newborn baby and had to wait for their machine to be installed.

She loves the job. "There's nothing that beats the smell of clean washing!" she says, adding her biggest satisfaction is seeing the players on TV run out with the cleanest kits!

Kiosks Manager Kerie Garwood does her final checks on all the eight Club kiosks before they open for business at 1.30pm. In fact, she's been in since 9am switching on all the equipment and making sure that there are enough burgers, hot dogs, pies and chips, ready for the rush.

Kerie, who used to be in the Army, finds her military experience useful in getting her staff of 26 organised for the busy day ahead.

Thirst-quenching: Kiosks Manager Kerie Garwood serves a fan from one of the County Ground's kiosks.

All the ordering is done during the week and she is familiar with what the fans want. The most popular fast snacks are burgers, followed by hot dogs and pies.

Pies were put on the menu by public demand. The kiosks even do vegetarian pies such as cheese and onion but one of the most popular hot snacks are chips.

Coffee and Bovril are also a big hit with fans. Bovril is really popular with the older generation of fans on a cold matchday.

Meanwhile over at the Executive suite, Bar Manager Graham Mulcahy checks everything's ready for the matchday rush.

He's been in for hours checking that all the bars in all the suites - from the Burmah suite to the supporters' lounge - are well stocked to quench the thirst of all the fans.

The bars have a pretty good mix of drinks - from Carling Black Label to Arkell's 3Bs and Worthington Bitter to the trendy designer beers like Sol and Becks.

"We want to make sure all the visitors have a good time. That's what coming to Swindon Town is all about," he said.

That's top priority with the Club's marketing team, too. Phil Alexander, Janet Garrett and their assistants Karlton St James and Justine Phillips are ready and waiting at around 1.30pm to personally receive guests to all the suites.

Janet and Justine give the sponsors a tour of the stadium

Getting the VIP treatment: Match sponsors and guests tour the ground before kick-off with Janet Garrett and her assistant Justine Phillips from the Club's marketing department.

On a matchday

1000 Burgers
800 Portions of chips
1500 Cups of coffee
800 Cups of tea
700 Cups of hot chocolate
400 Cups of soup
500 Cans of Coke
600 Mars Bars

are sold

BURGERS   CHIPS   COFFEE   TEA   CHOCOLATE   SOUP   COKE   MARS BARS

Improvements Fund.

At 1.30pm, Club physio Kevin Morris arrives. He has worked at the Club for 24 years and has got his routine down to a fine art.

The first thing he does is to check that his medical box and kit bag are equipped with everything and anything the players might need. From inflatable splints to aspirin - name it and Kevin's probably got it!

His field kit is in a small lightweight bag so he can run on the field if needed. "I need to be able to run out on the pitch at lightning speed to see to a player if he gets injured so I can't be weighed down. Time is of the essence in football and I can't waste a second," says Kevin.

At 1.45pm he reports to John Gorman and checks the players to see if they need anything before the match.

Kevin's been doing the job so long, that the briefing has just become a formality.

"I've got to know over the years what the players need - I haven't been caught out yet!" he said with a laugh.

The Club's GP, Dr John Nicholas, is also in attendance in case a player has an injury.

At 2.15pm Julie Page and Chris McLoughlin organise STFC's official cheerleaders, The Robinettes.

Formed at the beginning of last season, the girls, all from local schools, perform a dance routine at half-time in their

A grand draw: The half-time nest-egg promotion sellers Harold Cotton, left, and Robert Leighfield, far right, with promotions organiser Dave Hollister, 2nd left, and marketing controller Phil Alexander.

Fit for action: Team physio Kevin Morris with his medical kit.

while Phil and Karlton check on how the promotions team are doing.

Dave Hollister and Ralph Whiting make up the promotions team. The latest promotion is the nest-egg promotion which has been a huge success so far. Money raised from this and other competitions is going towards the Club's Ground

The young ones: Matchday mascots line-up for a day they will never forget.

colourful red outfits.

Dinner lady, Julie Page rehearses with them every Thursday after school. Julie has been a fan since she was three years-old and is now almost fifty.

At 2.30pm, the mascots arrive. These are children who have chosen to be mascots for the match. They meet in the Premier Lounge and are looked after by Mascot co-ordinator, George Chadwick. The children are given a kit which they put on when

Dancing queens: The Robinettes entertaining the fans with a half-time routine.

Sweeper system: The match is over and the crowds have gone - but the rubbish hasn't!

they arrive. They are then given a ball which they take round the dressing room for players to autograph.

The mascots are then taken down to the boot room ready to run out with the players and have their photographs taken just before the match.

Around the same time, the ballboys arrive. There are six in all and they are selected from the Junior Robins Supporters Club, which is run by the Club's Commercial department.

The ballboys for the day collect and return any stray ball that goes off the pitch. There are always six on matchday, situated at various points on different sides of the pitch. But, 15 minutes before the match starts, they are waiting either side of the tunnel ready to welcome the players.

At 3pm, the whistle goes, the countdown is over for another game and the match begins.

Ipswich Town 20.11.93. Home. 13,777

2-2

Swindon: Digby, Fenwick, Nijholt, Whitbread, Taylor, Bodin, Horlock, Summerbee, Moncur, Scott, Mutch. Subs Ling (for Summerbee), MacLaren.

5 All in the Game

Highlights of the 1993/94 season

New signing Keith Scott got a goal in his first outing for the Town, drawing the scores level at 1-1 shortly before half-time. Ipswich took the lead again through a penalty in the 63rd minute but Paul Bodin converted from the spot at the other end after a foul on Martin Ling. For Bodin the goal was especially sweet. Three days earlier he had missed a penalty for Wales which could have put them in the World Cup.

Queens Park Rangers 24.11.93. Home. 14,147

1-0

Swindon: Digby, Whitbread, Bodin, Nijholt, Taylor, Moncur, Ling, Horlock, Fenwick, Scott, Mutch. Subs Fjortoft, Maskell.

Paul Bodin in action against QPR.

"That Wembley feeling all over again," was how John Gorman described this historic victory - Swindon's first in the Premiership. What made the vital win all the more remarkable was that Swindon played with ten men for most of the game following Luc

Nijholt's 18th minute dismissal for foul language.

Keith Scott ended the Town's long and frustrating wait for a win with his crucial 50th minute goal.

Liverpool 11.12.93. Away. 32,739

2-2

Swindon: Digby, Moncur, Bodin, Whitbread, Taylor, Ling, Summerbee, Fenwick, Horlock, Scott, Mutch. Subs Fjortoft (for Moncur), Maskell (for Summerbee).

This game proved what many of the Town's fans had known for a long time - that Swindon could play the best teams in the country in the biggest grounds and hold their own. Many Liverpool fans leaving Anfield praised Swindon's stylish football, acknowledging the Town was the better side on the day.

The Town had twice taken the lead - first through John Moncur then with Keith Scott's third goal in six games - only to see Liverpool bounce back, their second equaliser coming just four minutes from time.

Southampton 18.12.93. Home. 13,284
2-1

Swindon: Digby, Whitbread, Bodin, Fenwick, Taylor, Moncur, Ling, Horlock, Maskell, Scott, Mutch. Subs Fjortoft, Berkley.

Paul Bodin received his 1992/93 cap before the game, then set out to destroy the Saints - first with a solo goal after 12 minutes, then with a corner which Scott headed home and finally with a shot cleared off the line. The influence of ex-England hit man Frank Worthington, brought in by John Gorman to sharpen up Swindon's attack in training, clearly showed.

Keith Scott silenced the Kop with Swindon's second goal at Anfield only to see Liverpool get a late equaliser.

Sheffield Wednesday 29.12.93. Away. 30,570
3-3

Swindon: Digby, Moncur, Summerbee, Whitbread, Taylor, Ling, Maskell, Fenwick, Horlock, Scott, Mutch. Subs MacLaren, Fjortoft (for Scott).

Craig Maskell's two goals against Sheffield Wednesday gave the Town a share of the points at Hillsborough.

Despite the 4-0 defeat at home against Arsenal on Boxing Day, the Swindon players kept their heads up for this difficult game at

Hillsborough which will be remembered for Wednesday's goal while Fraser Digby was grounded.

Swindon had twice taken the lead through goals by Mutch and Maskell but Wednesday pulled goals back both times and then led 3-2 until the final minute. But the Town players showed their mettle to fight back and get a valuable point when Maskell got his second in the 90th minute.

Coventry City 3.1.94. Away. 15,825
1-1

Swindon: Hammond, Moncur, Summerbee, Whitbread, Taylor, Ling, Maskell, Fenwick, Horlock, Bodin, Mutch. Subs Scott (for Maskell), MacLaren.

Again never-say-die Swindon fought back to grab a point through Andy Mutch's last-minute goal. Nicky Hammond played even though he was recovering from a bug. In the days prior to the game John Gorman and Dave Hay had made a frantic search for a keeper should he be too ill to play.

Tottenham Hotspur 22.1.94. Home. 16,563
2-1

Swindon: Hammond, Moncur, Summerbee, Whitbread, Taylor, Ling, Fjortoft, Nijholt, Horlock, Kilcline, Mutch. Subs Bodin (for Ling), Scott (for Mutch).

*Adrian Whitbread got the
winner against Spurs at the
County Ground when Swindon
outclassed Ossie Ardiles' side.*

Jan Aage Fjortoft and Adrian Whitbread scored their first league goals for Swindon to clinch an important victory against a Tottenham side managed by former Town boss Ossie Ardiles and featuring Colin Calderwood, Swindon ex-captain.

Swindon again proved they could command games against top sides. Spurs went ahead on the half-hour only for the Town to roar back and demolish the Londoners with new signing Brian 'Killer' Kilcline shoring up Swindon's defence.

Coventry City 5.2.94. Home. 14,640
3-1

Nicky Summerbee's performance against Coventry City helped the Town grab all three points with three goals.

Swindon: Hammond, Moncur, Summerbee, Whitbread, Taylor, Ling, Fjortoft, Nijholt, Horlock, Kilcline, Scott. Subs Bodin (for Ling), Maskell.

After re-discovering his goal-scoring ability in the Town's two previous games, Fjortoft put in a blistering performance to gun down the Sky Blues with his first hat-trick in English football and Swindon's first of the season. Two came from penalties.

Norwich City 19.2.94. Home. 15,405
3-3

Swindon: Sheffield, Summerbee, Bodin, Taylor, Kilcline, Nijholt, Horlock, Moncur, Whitbread, Fjortoft, Scott. Subs Hammond (for Sheffield), McAvennie (for Scott).

A six-goal thriller in which Norwich twice gained the lead only to see the Town come back, first from a Shaun Taylor shot and then from a Fjortoft header a minute before half-time. Fjortoft put Swindon into the lead in the 50th minute only to see Norwich come back in the 83rd minute to deny the Town all three points.

SWINDON TOWN FC FIXTURES 1993/94

Date	Opponents	F	A	Att.	1 DIGBY	2 SUMMERBEE	3 BODIN	4 HAZARD	5 NIJHOLT	6 TAYLOR	7 MONCUR	8 MacLAREN	9 FJORTOFT	10 LING	11 MASKELL	12 WHITE	13 WHITBREAD	14 VIVEASH	15 HORLOCK	16 HAMON	17 MURRAY	18 THOMSON	19 O'SULLIVAN	20 PHILLIPS	21 BERKLEY	22 HAMMOND	23 MIDDLETON	24 MUTCH	25 FENWICK	26 SCOTT	27 GOODEN	28 COOK	29 KERR	30 KILCLINE	31 SHEFFIELD	40
Sat 14 Aug	Sheffield United	A	1-3	20,904	•	•		•	•	❶	•	•	•	•	•	•	○	S			○															
Wed 18 Aug	Oldham Athletic	H	0-1	11,940	•	•		•	•	•	•	•	•	•	•	○	○	S			○		•													
Sun 22 Aug	Liverpool	H	0-5	17,017	•	•	S	•	•	•	•	•	S		•		•				○		•													
Wed 25 Aug	Southampton	A	1-5	12,581	•	•	S	•	•	•	•	•	S1		•		•				○		•													
Sat 28 Aug	Norwich City	A	0-0	17,614	•	•		•	•	•	•	S	•	S		•		•				○		•													
Wed 1 Sep	Manchester City	H	1-3	16,067	•	❶		•	•	•	•	S	•	S		•		•				○		•													
Sat 11 Sep	West Ham United	A	0-0	15,777	•	•		•	•	•	•		•	•	S	•		•				○		•	S												
Sat 18 Sep	Newcastle United	H	2-2	15,015	•	•	•	•	•	•		•	❶		S	•						○		•	S												
Wed 22 Sep	Wolverhampton W.C.C.C 2 (1)	H	2-0	8,649	•	❶	•	•	•	•	○		•	○	•							○		❶	•												
Sat 25 Sep	Manchester United	A	2-4	44,583	•	•	❶	•	•	•		S	•	•	S							○		❶	•												
Sat 2 Oct	Blackburn Rovers	H	1-3	15,224	•	•	•	•	•	❶	•	S	S	•	•									•	❶	•											
Tue 5 Oct	Wolverhampton W.C.C.C 2 (2)	A	1-2	15,756	○	❶	•	•	•	•	•		○	•	S									•	❶	•											
Sat 16 Oct	Everton	H	1-1	14,437	•	•	•		•	❶	•	S	•	•			S					○		•	•												
Sat 23 Oct	Tottenham Hotspur	A	1-1	31,394	•	•	❶		•	•	•	•	•	○			S					○		•	•												
Tue 26 Oct	Portsmouth (C.C.C 3)	A	0-2	12,554	•	•	•		•	•	•	•		S			S					○		•	•												
Sat 30 Oct	Aston Villa	H	1-2	16,322	•	•	❶		•	•	•		S		S							○		•	•												
Sat 6 Nov	Wimbledon	A	0-3	7,758	•	•		•	•	•	•	•	•	S	S	•						○		•													
Sat 20 Nov	Ipswich Town	H	2-2	13,860	•	•	❶		•	•	•	S		S	○	•		•				○		•	•	❶										
Wed 24 Nov	Queens Park Rangers	H	1-0	14,147	•		•		•	•	•	○	•	○		•		•				○		•	•	❶										
Sat 27 Nov	Leeds United	A	0-3	32,630	•		•		•	•	•	○	S	•		•		•				○		•	•	❶										
Sat 4 Dec	Sheffield United	H	0-0	12,882	•	S	•		•	•	•			•	S		•					○		•	•	•										
Tue 7 Dec	Oldham Athletic	A	1-2	9,771	•	•	•		•	•	•		○	○		•		•				○		•	•	•										
Sat 11 Dec	Liverpool	A	2-2	32,739	•	•	•			•	❶		S	•	S	•						○		❶	•	•										
Sat 18 Dec	Southampton	H	2-1	13,284	•		❶		•	•		○	•	•		•					○	○		•	•	❶										
Mon 27 Dec	Arsenal	H	0-4	17,651	•	S	•		•	•		S	•	•		•						○		•	•	•										
Wed 29 Dec	Sheffield Wednesday	A	3-3	30,570	•	•			•	•	○	S	•	❷		•						S		❶	•	•										
Sat 1 Jan	Chelsea	H	1-3	16,456		•	S		•	•		S	•	•		•						•		❶	•	•		○								
Mon 3 Jan	Coventry City	A	1-1	15,825		•	•		•	•	○		•	•		•						•		❶	•	S		○								
Sat 8 Jan	Ipswich Town (FAC 3)	H	1-1	12,105		•	•	S	•	•		S	•	•		•						•		❶	•			○								
Sat 15 Jan	Everton	A	2-6	20,546		•	❶	S	•	❶		S	•			•						•		❶	•		•		○							
Tue 18 Jan	Ipswich Town (FAC 3R)	A	1-2*	12,796		•	•		•	•	○	❶	•	S		•						•		•	•	•			○							
Sat 22 Jan	Tottenham Hotspur	H	2-1	16,568		•	S		•	•	•	○	❶	•			❶		•			•		•		S		○	•							
Sat 5 Feb	Coventry City	H	3-1	14,635		•	S		•	•	•	❸	•	○		•		•				•		•					•	○						
Sat 12 Feb	Aston Villa	A	0-5	26,637		•	S		•	•	•		•	•		•		•				○		S	•				•	•						
Sat 19 Feb	Norwich City	H	3-3	15,405		•	•		•	❶	•	❷	○			•		•				S			•				•	•						
Sat 26 Feb	Manchester City	A																																	
Sat 5 Mar	West Ham United	H																																	
Sat 12 Mar	Newcastle United	A																																		
Sat 19 Mar	Manchester United	H																																		
Sat 26 Mar	Blackburn Rovers	A																																		
Sat 2 Apr	Arsenal	A																																		
Mon 4 Apr	Sheffield Wednesday	H																																		
Sat 9 Apr	Chelsea	A																																		
Sat 16 Apr	Ipswich Town	A																																		
Sat 23 Apr	Wimbledon	H																																		
Sat 30 Apr	Queens Park Rangers	A																																		
Sat 7 May	Leeds United	H																																		

*After extra time

53

Burmah

6 To be the Boss

Four Swindon Town managers talk about their time at the Town

JOHN GORMAN
1993 to present

IF awards for the most popular person in football were handed out John Gorman would have a cupboard full.

For John has played with or against most of the soccer greats of the last 30 years - and has become firm friends with all of them.

Such popularity may be rare in football but it is all part and parcel of John's attitude to the game.

John grew up in a mining village just outside Edinburgh where every boy dreamed of being a footballer.

"I was no different!" he says. "I lived, breathed and would even have eaten football if I could!"

At the age of 15 the dream came true for John. He joined Celtic, the club he worshipped as a boy, as an apprentice and found himself rubbing shoulders with soccer legends.

Even the team-sheets for the reserves,

which John played in for five years, read like a who's who of Scottish soccer.

Lou Macari, Kenny Dalglish and David Hay were team mates who became great friends. "We had football in common and were hungry for the game - we lived and breathed it!" says John.

John moved south of the border to Carlisle for £12,000 in 1970 and made 200 appearances for the club in the First and Second Divisions, mainly playing fullback.

In 1976 Spurs manager Keith Burkinshaw bought him for £80,000 and John joined a talented squad which included Glenn Hoddle and Ossie Ardiles.

But after 16 games he tore a ligament in his left knee - an injury which was effectively to end his playing career in England.

An operation put him on the road to recovery only for Burkinshaw to tell him his playing days were over. But John had no intention of hanging up his boots at the age of 29 and went to America to play with the Tampa Bay Rowdies where he was to stay for four years.

In 1983 he went on to play with the Phoenix Indoor Team until the club folded two years later.

He headed back to England - and to Gillingham where he was given the opportunity to coach and play with the reserve team with Keith Peacock. In 1987 at the age of 37, he made two appearances with Gillingham's first team.

"I was the oldest player at Gillingham ever to make his debut!" joked John. "I really enjoyed my time there. It gave me my first taste of coaching - seeing football from a side other than as a player.

"I enjoyed coaching the younger players. It certainly helped me later on when I entered management" - a move he made in 1988 to become reserve team manager with Orient.

Even then he still turned out for the side. "It was great. I had entered management with all the responsibility that brings, but I was also able to play. Every footballer wants to play forever.

"I knew the time would come when I would have to stop, but

at Orient I had the best of both worlds."

John had kept in touch with Glenn Hoddle after leaving Spurs, visiting him in Monaco. "That's the way it is in football - once you make a friend, you never lose touch, no matter where your career takes you." said John.

It was while at Orient that John got the call to come to Swindon. He had applied for the manager's job at Carlisle and had asked Glenn to write him a recommendation. Instead Glenn phoned with the offer to join him at Swindon.

"He said: 'Come with me to Swindon - we'll make a great team'. How could I refuse an offer like that? I had a lot of respect for the Club. It had a smell of success about it. I knew going with Glenn was the right thing to do."

And it was. So began the start of what John describes as two wonderful years.

"We were very close and had no disagreements. That's the way it should work. You can't have a successful partnership without that. There has got to be an atmosphere of trust. A close relationship like that can't work without it," said John.

He got to know and enjoy working in Swindon. "I knew it the minute I came that Swindon was my kind of town. It was like a second home to me."

He also grew to love the fans and their loyalty to the Club - a loyalty he was beginning to share. That loyalty was put to the test when, shortly after promotion to the Premiership, Glenn announced he was leaving to go to Chelsea as manager and asked John to go as his number two.

John accepted the offer. He told the directors of his decision, packed his bags and literally was about to walk out the door after having said his goodbyes, when the Town Chairman Ray Hardman approached him.

"Glenn had said all his goodbyes but had forgotten to speak to Jean, our laundry lady. I reminded him and he went to say farewell," remembers John.

"I collected the last of my things, when Ray asked if he could have a word with me. He said he wanted me to stay as manager. I told him I needed time to think."

On the way to pick up his son from training, John realised what a golden opportunity he had been offered. The chance to be his own man. He also thought of what he was turning down - the chance to be number two to a man who was on his way to the top.

He decided on that drive he would stay. He phoned Glenn and met him on the motorway. "Glenn

was upset but told me that, ultimately it was my decision," said John.

The fans, directors and players were all delighted at John's decision. But as a manager John faced fresh challenges, not least of which were negotiations with players over contracts and the departure of Colin Calderwood, the Town's long-serving skipper and the last player from their Fourth Division days.

Within days John had appointed his old Celtic colleague David Hay as his assistant. Unlike John, David had secured a first-team place at Celtic and made 200 appearances, gaining five Scottish League Championship medals, two Scottish Cup and one League Cup.

He also played more than 100 times for Chelsea after being transferred to Stamford Bridge in 1974 and was capped 27 times for Scotland. He managed Celtic for four seasons, St Mirren for two and was assistant manager at Motherwell and Watford as well as working twice in the US.

"David was my one and only choice for the job. We trust and respect each other. We've been in the game a long time and have been great friends along the way," says John. John and David decided the style of football which had won the Club promotion, and many admirers, under Glenn would stay.

There was also some money to buy players and the pair developed an eye for a bargain. Before the start of the season Luc Nijholt, Jan Aage Fjortoft and Adrian Whitbread joined the squad; Keith Scott brought more strike power when he was signed a few weeks into the season; Terry Fenwick brought a wealth of experience to midfield and Brian 'Killer' Kilcline made a rock solid addition to defence after joining in January.

Having got into the hot seat at last, John is enjoying every minute of it, backed up by his own team at home - wife Myra who goes to all away matches, daughter Amanda, 20, and son Nicholas, 17.

"When I'm not at work, I'm still working," he says. "I can't leave the job behind. It's with you all the time. But I've always been that way. Football is my passion.

"It's like a drug to me. I can't switch off. I miss playing, but being a manager is the next best thing."

It was Town Chairman Ray Hardman who, literally at the last minute, got John to stay at the Club.

Hay on Gorman

"He is the most supportive manager and the best friend anyone could ever have. With John you know where you are and I'm proud to know him."

The longest half-hour in the Town's history

// A few days after the victory at Wembley, Glenn and John told us of their decision to leave. We were stunned. We knew Glenn would eventually go because he was a superstar, but not as quickly as that," said Ray.

"Most managers when they go, take their assistants with them - so I knew that persuading John to stay would be difficult. The relationship between John and Glenn was very strong."

But Ray was determined to to try.

Burmah's Managing Director Rikki Hunt had tipped Ray off that the pair were coming in to say their final farewells.

Rikki had spent several hours in long discussions with both Glenn and John, in turn, in a final attempt to convince them they should stay together as a team with Swindon Town.

"They both came to my office and I spent several hours trying to persuade them to change their minds. It was obvious to me that

Burmah

Portrait of the artist as a young man. John Gorman's self-portrait, painted while a player in the US, shows a hidden talent.

Glenn's mind was made up, but John's was not. I felt that a final chat with Ray would persuade John to stay. The rest is history "

After Rikki's tip-off, Ray played his final card - and it proved to be a winner.

"I spent half-an-hour persuading him. It was the longest half-hour in history," remembers Ray.

"It wasn't that he didn't want to - he was torn. Torn between his desire to stay with Glenn and keep up a successful partnership as well as a friendship or remain with the Club that I knew he had grown to love.

"I wasn't alone in my wish that he stay. All the directors wanted John to stay on as manager and the fans had grown to love him. I had absolutely no doubt in my mind that John was right to manage Swindon.

"While Glenn had done an incredible amount for the Club, keeping Swindon in Divsion Two in the first season and then getting into the Premiership, John had been the unsung hero.

"Glenn was and is a superstar - there is no doubt in my mind about that - but I knew one day he would go. It was just a matter of time. When he announced his decision to leave, all the directors knew the Club had to have

continuity. That continuity was John.

"It really was a last-minute plea. In fact, it was at the 11th hour and 59th minute! He was overwhelmed. I could see he really was!

"It was tough for John. But he did stay and I'm very glad he did! John is one of the nicest people you could hope to meet, he's good with the players and always has time for the fans.

"That dramatic half-hour was time well spent!" said Ray with a smile.

◆◆◆◆◆◆◆

GLENN HODDLE 1991-1993

GLENN Hoddle's appointment as Swindon Town manager nearly never happened. The gifted former Spurs and England international was about to turn out for his first game in 20 months when his phone rang.

The game was for Chelsea reserves. Glenn had used the club's training facilities to get back into shape after a serious knee injury ended his spell with French club Monaco.

He was considering signing with Chelsea as a player if his injury healed completely or possibly as a youth team coach if it didn't.

"I nearly didn't answer the phone!" said Glenn. "It was around 12 o'clock with the game due to start at two and I was literally walking out the door."

The call was from Peter Day, then Swindon Town's chief executive. "Peter popped the question and I said I needed to think about it. But it was a great opportunity and I thought why not?

There comes a stage in every player's career when they have to decide where they go next," said Glenn.

"After 20 months out, I wondered whether my career as a player was finished and I had thought of coaching or management as my next step. I thought managing Swindon was right so I went along to see Peter and we did the deal."

When Glenn accepted the offer, he told Chelsea of his plans.

They wished him well, little knowing he would be back there two years later as manager. "It's funny the way things work out!" said Glenn with a laugh.

Glenn and Swindon realised they were both stepping into the unknown. "I had never managed a Club and I couldn't play, and at that time I didn't know whether I would ever be able to play again, so they were taking a chance on me," he said.

 Burmah

"I'll always be grateful to them for giving me the chance. They wanted a manager and never at any point did Peter Day put pressure on me to play. At that time, I didn't know if I ever would but that didn't matter to them.

"My knee did heal and I knew when it was right to play again and the rest is history."

The First Division play-offs seemed a long way away when Glenn first walked through the gates at the County Ground.

He signed his contract on Wednesday. On Thursday he started his new job as manager of a Second Division side with a match to play on Saturday.

The Club and its fans were still smarting from the relegation punishment at the end of the previous season and a run of poor performances on the field had hit morale.

The Town lost its first match with Glenn as manager but it was hardly suprising. With barely two days there was no time for him to make any changes.

The first week was the most unbelievable experience for Glenn and something he will never forget.

"I thought: 'Hang on - it can't always be like this'. There were so many things to do and so many decisions to make. No day was the same and it was entirely different to being a player."

One of the things he did introduce was the sweeper system -

a style he had always favoured as a player. It was a bold move, according to Glenn, bearing in mind the financial constraints and the threat of relegation. Many would not have tried something so radical so soon.

But Glenn felt it was right. His 20 months out of the game had changed his view of football. He had spent a lot of time watching football on TV and it gave him a different perspective on the game from being a player.

In his first full season as manager Swindon finished eighth - just two places outside the play-offs. It was the frustration in the squad that spurred Glenn on.

"I was disappointed for the players who had played some marvellous games that season - for myself and John (Gorman, his assistant) for the work we had put in."

Glenn also had to sell players, something he was not keen to do, but knew had to be done. The financial constraints of the Club at the time meant decisions on buying and selling had to be the right ones.

Glenn strengthened the side with a string of bargain signings - John Moncur for £80,000, Dave Mitchell for £30,000 and Martin Ling for just £10,000. They all paid-off and looking back on it now Glenn rates buying players like these as among his happiest memories of Swindon.

"Getting into the Premiership obviously was also a proud moment - not only for me but the players and the fans," he said.

"Let's face it, football changes, players change, managers change but the fans remain the same. They are loyal and stick with their team. If you're a Swindon Town supporter when you're five,

Hoddle on Gorman

"There are some people you just get on with right from the start and John was one of them. The chemistry was there from the moment we met - we gelled.

"John was with Orient at the time and the first thing I did as manager was to bring John to Swindon. He was the first and only choice for me.

"I remember saying to John when he was staying with me and the family when I was with Monaco that if I got a team, I would want to bring him with me if he wanted to come. His response at the time was that he would love to come."

The closeness between the two is apparent when Glenn says:"John is a wonderful person, brilliant coach and excellent manager. He is without doubt one of the most gifted managers and genuine people in football.

"As a coach he is the most professional I know - he would spend hours with players. As a person, I couldn't ask for a better friend. He's more like family to me than a friend. He's a smashing guy.

"We were a good team at Swindon. We could tell each other anything. Being friends and trusting each other helped.

"His fiery temperament matched my calmer one perfectly. He is passionate about the game. Swindon Town is very lucky to have him.

"I was sad that he didn't come with me, but in the end the decision had to be his and not mine. I am happy for him and we're still as close as we've always been. John's like that - he never loses a friend."

Glenn Hoddle, flanked by
police, returns to the County
Ground as Chelsea manager.

you'll still be a fan of the Club when you're sixty.

"One of my proudest and memorable moments at the Town was seeing the looks on their faces when we knew we'd done it for them. That's something I'll always remember of my time with the Town."

Of the play-off final: "I always knew we'd do it. I was a little bit worried when we went from 3-0 to 3-3, but I had known from the early part of the season that we'd get there."

As well as bringing Premiershop football to Swindon, Glenn also brought John Gorman. The two first met when they played together at Tottenham and according to Glenn, clicked right from the start.

Looking back, Glenn says that his decision to leave was made when the Club had to sell David Kerslake.

He remembers saying: 'Well, here we go again. Is the carpet going to be pulled from under us again?'

"I did understand the reasons behind the sale. Financial con-straints meant the directors had to make the decision to sell. I know if they had had the money, it wouldn't have happened.

"They are a smashing bunch of guys and good businessmen. The sale helped the Club at the time. I understood why it had to be done, but as a player-manager it was very frustrating.

"So, I think at the back of my mind I thought if a chance comes up, I'll take it. It wasn't an immediate 'I'll go at the end of the season' thing. More like 'If a chance comes up, do what your mind says - not what your heart tells you'."

That chance came in the shape of Chelsea with the offer of the manager's job and few financial constraints.

"It was a bit sad, because people thought I had let them down at the time.

"The last day was very emotional for me - my heart was telling me to stay, but my head was saying something else. As I was saying goodbye, all sorts of feelings and memories were running through my head. It was a difficult, emotional time.

"I loved my time with the Club and the challenges it presented me with as a new first-time manager and the loyalty of the fans.

"You never forget your first time at anything. I remember my first match with Tottenham at 11 and I'll never forget the first Club I managed. No matter where I go or what I do, those memories will always be with me. I learnt a lot during my time at Swindon.

"It's a lovely Club, a great team of directors and good staff with the most loyal crowd of fans.

"For me, it gave me the chance to make the transition from player to manager and the experience to deal with all types of people from Jean the laundry lady to the Board which I thoroughly enjoyed.

"Scouting for players, combined with training for matches. I had to deal with all that, but I'm not complaining. Swindon Town gave me the chance to do that. They took a chance on me.

"I feel that the team up to the end of my time gave the fans entertainment value."

He was surprised at the strength of feeling towards him when he returned to the County Ground with Chelsea - feelings he puts down to Swindon's position at the foot of the Premiership.

"But that's football!" he said.

OSSIE ARDILES 1989-1991

A GIFTED player who had won a World Cup winners' medal with Argentina, Ossie Ardiles will go down in history as Swindon's unluckiest manager.

He came to Swindon at the age of 37 after an illustrious career as a player. He had decided that the time had come to give up playing but wanted to stay in football.

"Being a manager was the next best thing," he said. He was approached by the then-Chairman of Swindon Brian Hillier.

He played a couple of games with Swindon but decided to hang up his boots when he realised his efforts would be better channelled behind the manager's desk.

"Everyone knows when their time is up," said Ossie. "Some don't want to admit it. I did. I just wanted to concentrate on being a manager."

Ossie had trained to be a lawyer in his native Argentina before entering professional football. It is ironic that his time at

Swindon was soured by the illegal payments scandal and Swindon's promotion, then demotion and eventual re-appointment to the Second Division.

The transition to manager was a slight shock for Ossie, but he quickly got used to it. Picking teams, training and scouting quickly became second nature to him.

He loved his time with Swindon, his most memorable moment was winning the play-off final at Wembley.

"The supporters who turned out to cheer us warmed my heart. It was wonderful to see them in such numbers at the match," he said.

It seemed that even the soccer-mad Argentinians had nothing on the devotion of Swindon fans. "There were over 40,000. I had never seen anything like it. It wasn't like that in my country.

"The warmth of Swindon people was something I will never forget."

Ossie kept on Lou Macari's assistant Chic Bates. "You can't bring in totally new people. We didn't have the money to do that. I concentrated my financial resources on the players. Chic was a good Deputy. Why change a successful formula?"

Ossie also changed Swindon's style of play from Macari's long-ball technique to a gentle South American-style passing game.

Ossie Ardiles in pensive mood during his return to Swindon as Tottenham boss.

But he continued Macari's habit of discovering top class players and buying them on the cheap. David Kerslake was snapped up from QPR for £110,000.

Ossie also loved the town, and misses Marlborough where he lived while manager.

"It was beautiful.

"My time there was happy. It was my first time as a manager and it taught me a lot. I'll never forget Swindon Town."

64

LOU MACARI 1984-89

WHEN he took on the job as The Boss at Swindon Town, Lou Macari was 34 with a glittering career in football behind him.

He had played for Celtic in his native Glasgow, had made more than 400 appearances for Manchester United and scored over 100 goals, and been capped for Scotland.

He wasn't injured, burnt-out or tired of the game. He just wanted to be a manager. It was to Swindon's advantage that he did so at the time when the Club was not only struggling in the Fourth Division but also manager-less.

"People did wonder why I was going from the First Division to the Fourth!" he said with a laugh. "But the time was right for me to make the move. It wasn't an easy decison and one that wasn't forced on me because I wasn't injured and was playing with a top club. But I knew the time was right."

The Swindon Town job had been advertised in the Daily Mail. Derby County was also looking for a manager at the same time and Lou went for both. Swindon made a firm offer first and so he headed towards Wiltshire for the start of the 1984/85 season.

His open, forthright manner came as a breath of fresh air to the Club. His first task was to build up a team of players and get them fit.

Lou Macari, now at Celtic, took the Town from the depths of the Fourth Division to the threshold of the First.

65

"Fitness was, and is, the way to get a top team. If the players aren't fit, how can you get the best out of them?" says Lou. "That was the philosophy I applied and it seemed to work."

Although Lou had joined as player-manager, he soon dropped out of playing and concentrated on building up the squad. He spent a lot of time scouting and bought many players at bargain basement prices, including Fraser Digby and Alan McLoughlin from his old club Manchester United, Paul Bodin from Newport County, Colin Calderwood from Mansfield Town, Duncan Shearer from Huddersfield and Fitzroy Simpson, who was recruited locally.

Lou now looks back on his time with the Town with fondness - particularly buying players who then developed, usually to be sold for a big profit. Lou remembers going to Newport on a cold winter's evening to watch Paul Bodin play, then buying him for £25,000. The Welsh international was later sold for £550,000 to Crystal Palace.

Colin Calderwood, who became the first player to captain a team from the Fourth to First Division, was bought for £25,000 and sold last year for £1.25m.

Lou loved the job, stayed five-and-a-half years and took Swindon to its first Championship title - the Fourth Division - in his second season with a record 102 points; into the Second Division in his third season; and to the brink of the First Division in his last.

Lou became a hero in Swindon and a respected manager in the profession. Since leaving Swindon he has managed West Ham, Birmingham City, Stoke and Celtic with varying degrees of success.

"At Swindon I had to build up a team from scratch with the limited resources that a Fourth Division club had to offer. I learnt how to use my money wisely," says Lou.

"I've never had to do that anywhere again, but I enjoyed scouting and learnt how to buy wisely. It takes more skill with less money than with more."

Lou's success with Swindon made him a target for better-off clubs looking for a manager. But he rejected all offers. It was only

Macari on Gorman

Lou and John first met in 1969 when they were both teenagers playing in the Youth team of Celtic.

"John is a man who takes his job as manager very seriously," said Lou. "Swindon are lucky to have him. He is also a first rate player and coach and a very good friend.

"He has taken on a big job to keep Swindon in the Premiership, but did an even bigger job helping the Club to get there."

when it was widely reported in footballing circles that he had no ambition that he decided to go.

"I loved the Club, the people and the staff," says Lou. "They were great and it was a fantastic learning experience for me. The challenges of building a great team was a great experience and I take a great pride in the players I bought, who then went on to be sold at a much better price, bringing money into the Club.

"It was an experience I will never forget. Because of Swindon, I was able to go on to bigger and better things. I couldn't have done it without the Town."

Lou is also full of admiration for John Trollope, who became his assistant after the bizarre sacking and re-instatement of Lou and his first assistant Harry Gregg.

"John was perfect. He was loved by the fans, was a man with real talent, patience and his calm, cool temperament was a perfect match to me," says Lou. "When he asked to return to the youth team after two years I was sorry to lose him."

Lou's last game in charge at Swindon was the play-off defeat against Crystal Palace. The dream of taking the Town from the depths of the Fourth Division to the First had eluded Lou. But the Club he left to go to West Ham was far stronger than when he joined.

7 The Driving Force behind Swindon Town

Burmah Petroleum Fuels - a Company that's going places.

JUNE 1991 was a very special time in Swindon Town's history. Burmah Petroleum Fuels became the Club's main sponsor, pledging £500,000 over three years and so lifting a huge burden off its financial situation.

"And to think it was all down to one football match!" said Managing Director Rikki Hunt, whose idea it was to team-up Club and Company. "If I hadn't gone, and it was a last-minute thing, Burmah wouldn't be involved now."

Burmah Petroleum Fuels had placed an advertising board at the County Ground and as a result Rikki had been invited to attend a pre-season friendly against Real Sociadad.

Rikki, a dyed-in-the-wool Liverpool fan, was impressed with the Town's style of play - but noticed Swindon didn't have any advertising on their shirts.

"I mentioned it to the Chief Executive and he said the Club couldn't get anyone interested because of the recent tax problems," said Rikki.

"I was amazed! Here was a Club that was on its way up, playing open and exciting football under the leadership of a well-known player-manager, Glenn Hoddle - and no-one was prepared to back them."

After the match, all sorts of questions were running through Rikki's mind.

For a start, no other fuel company was involved in football sponsorship. Market research had shown that football was popular with Burmah's target market and there was a lot of potential media coverage.

The next day, Rikki compared the Swindon away matches with a regional map of Burmah's service stations. To his amazement, there were only three areas where the company had no sites. All the more remarkable was that with promotion to the Premiership there would be no gaps at all.

"A pretty good fit by anybody's standards," laughs Rikki. He had considered two other Clubs - Sheffield Wednesday and Wimbledon - but neither came close to Swindon's potential.

Within ten days of visiting the County Ground the deal had been struck. Rikki finalised the sponsorship deal after a meeting with Glenn Hoddle, and Peter Day and Ken Chapman, the Chief Executive and Chairman at the time.

For both the Club and Rikki, it was a masterstroke. Rikki had only just joined Burmah and had suddenly signed a deal which would raise its profile considerably.

Rikki Hunt with fellow Swindon Town directors: left to right, Ray Hardman, Chairman, Cliff Puffett, John Archer, Sir Seton Wills and Mike Spearman, Vice-Chairman.

ibility of being supported by the largest independent fuel supplier in the UK.

The excitement at the Club had impressed Rikki. But he was also aware of the disorganisation behind the scenes and knew he had to look after Burmah's money by using his commercial expertise. This in turn, he knew would help the Club.

Some of his top staff visited the County Ground offices to help out. "They were there on-and-off, mainly in their own time for several months. And they had their own jobs at Burmah to do as well!" said Rikki.

The cost of the extra work would have come to many thousands of pounds   if theClub had brought in consultants.

Burmah Castrol House. Burmah staff were made available to Swindon Town for marketing and financial advice.

For the Club, the deal spelt the end of financial insecurity that had plagued it on an almost daily basis for years.

The speed at which the deal was arrived at was no suprise to anyone that knew Rikki. He had been headhunted by Burmah from Elf where he had been Marketing Manager to become the youngest Managing Director in the industry.

His instincts led him to believe that the teaming up of Burmah and Swindon Town would be a good commercial partnership. One immediate benefit was that with Burmah's money flowing in, the Club was able to buy Paul Bodin.

But pumping in cash wasn't all Burmah did. Almost immediately, Rikki made his staff available to the Club to give it much-needed financial and marketing advice along with the cred-

Burmah

Right *Rikki Hunt presents Swindon Town's hat-trick hero Jan Aage Fjortoft with the match ball after the 3-1 win over Coventry.*

But as the Burmah slogan is: "Together we'll do it," Rikki applied the same approach to the Club.

"I didn't just want to hand over the money and not know what was happening to it. A lot of sponsors do this and are happy. But that is just not Burmah's way," said Rikki.

Stuart Mac of GWR gets Rikki Hunt's views on a match at the County Ground.

matic, still altered the Club's image for the better. The team coach was painted in Swindon Town and Burmah colours. Even the room where players are interviewed before and after a match was redecorated by Burmah to make it more upmarket and suit the Club's new image.

The Burmah Suite entertains executives from the Company and its suppliers and major customers, giving Burmah the chance to say thank you to key people from inside and outside the Company. Some 1,100 people from all over the country have enjoyed a buffet lunch before watching the match over the past two seasons.

"It has worked tremendously well, and been a great source of corporate entertaining for us," said Rikki.

Six months after signing the sponsorship deal, Rikki was invited onto the Board as an associate Director - an appointment the local business community welcomed.

He is full of admiration for the directors. They recognised the marketing and financial advice brought in by a large company was something money couldn't buy.

"They could have kept us at arm's length, but didn't!" said Rikki.

Chairman Ray Hardman said: "When we first met, I knew

He also set about helping to restructure the Club's financial department, anxious that the Club should not face the spectre of insolvency as it had so many times before.

A financial controller was brought in. Prior to his appointment, occasional accounts were produced outside the Club. This information was spasmodic as well as costly.

But there were other changes which, although not as drawe'd have a close working relationship. I just did not know how close it would become."

Rikki attends every Board meeting, despite his own busy schedule at Burmah, and can be heard cheering on the team at every home match. But it's from his seat in the Burmah area- not his Board seat.

"I'm still working on matchday - entertaining Burmah customers, and I can't do it from my Board seat!" he said.

The partnership between Swindon Town and Burmah has not been all one way, though. The firm has benefited greatly through a higher profile and increased brand awareness.

Getting into the Premiership obviously gave the deal a huge boost. Swindon matches are now reported in all national papers while highlights are shown on national TV.

The last point is important for Burmah. The company did not have the resources to stage a major TV advertising campaign in the same way as its rivals - but now its name is seen most Saturday nights on the BBC.

Aside from the national publicity for Burmah, there has also been the local pride associated with Swindon Town's success.

Burmah sees itself as very much part of the community in Swindon. It not only has its head office in the town but also recruits most of its staff locally. As such it believes it has a duty to put something back into the community - and it does that through Swindon Town, amongst other things.

Although Rikki says the deal is about business, he has great affection for the Club, going to most away matches even though

A close working relationship. STFC Chairman Ray Hardman and Rikki Hunt.

Left *Burmah Petroleum Fuels Finance and Systems Director Chris McGowan presents Nicky Summerbee with January's Burmah Player of the Month Award.*

71

Sign of the times. Burmah used the electronic Wembley scoreboard at the play-off final to good effect.

Right Rikki Hunt meets Burmah service station dealer Dolores Duddy during a site visit to County Omagh, Northern Ireland.

with a logo which incorporates the Chinthe, the mythical Burmese lion. All its service stations will soon feature the new, distinctive, image.

Rikki is happy about the commercial relationship between the Company and Swindon Town and knows it will continue to be a prosperous one for both parties.

"It beats giving away glasses!" he said with a laugh.

he has a hectic business schedule. He has a close working relationship with John Gorman and is often consulted in key decisions affecting the squad, including player signings. He has brought his own vision to the Club in the same way he has done at Burmah. He keeps as close as possible to the people who make the firm tick - the dealers in its 1,200 service stations.

Although they are spread around the country, Rikki makes sure that he and the rest of the Burmah Board of Directors visit sites once a week. In the two-and-a half years that Rikki has been in charge, over 700 sites have had a personal visit from a Director.

Burmah, the largest independent fuel supplier and fifth biggest oil company in the UK, now has a strong brand image

REWARD

REWARD, launched by Burmah almost two years ago, has been a huge hit with dealers and their customers.

The idea behind REWARD is simple. When Burmah customers buy petrol they are given a 'smart' card on which points can be collected every time they buy fuel at a Burmah service station.

The points can then be exchanged for goods from three major retailers - Comet, B&Q and Index or for an instant gift such as a video cassette. The unique aspect of this promotion is that points collected can be donated as cash to any of three charities - Save the Children, Age Concern and the RSPCA. The Burmah customer has a choice. It seems that the charities are winning. Almost 10,000 donations have been made since REWARD was launched.

"The REWARD promotion is popular because the customer can give to charities positively and not just drop the card in a box," said Rikki Hunt, Burmah Petroleum Fuels Managing Director.

The charities write personally to each customer who makes a donation. The promotion has been so popular that Burmah will be running it for a long while yet.

The "Chinthe Device" is a registered trademark of Burmah Castrol Plc. "Burmah" is a trademark of Burmah Castrol Trading Ltd. and Burmah Petroleum Fuels Ltd.

8 The Future

A glimpse into the future of Swindon Town on field and off.

AMBITIOUS plans for the future of Swindon Town are being made both on-and-off the field.

The exciting times that lie ahead will not only see a wealth of new playing talent emerge from the Club's youth and reserve sides, but they will face their opposition in a stadium ready for the 21st century.

In line with the Taylor Report, the County Ground has to become all-seater from the start of the 1994/95 season.

That has given the Club the unique opportunity of developing two new stands to replace the Stratton Bank and the Shrivenham Road stand.

Stratton Bank will become a 3,600 all-seater covered stand while Shrivenham Road will be a 5,000 seater, also covered.

Up to £2m is to come from the Football Trust towards the work, which is due to start straight after the Town's last game of the season against Leeds on 7 May.

Money is also being raised from a variety of sources including local companies.

Swindon Town Chairman Ray Hardman said: "The fans deserve to have stands with the most up-to-date facilities and we're going to try our hardest to make it happen!"

Equally important to the Club is the Youth Team, from which budding Keith Scotts, Shaun Taylors and Nicky Summerbees will be plucked.

The team operates under the watchful eye of John Trollope MBE, a Town veteran who played in the 1969 giant-killing League Cup Final against Arsenal at Wembley

Right The shape of things to come. New stands are planned for the Stratton bank and Shrivenham Road, top left and right on this model of the new County Ground.

Club Chairman Ray Hardman: "The fans deserve up-to-date facilities."

and still holds the record for the highest number of appearances for one club.

John, who has been with the Club for 34 years, started out as an apprentice and had to do the type of jobs such as getting the kits ready and cleaning the dressing rooms which he now makes sure the current youngsters do.

In his first season with the Club, he played in the Reserve Team with Nicky Summerbee's father, Mike who went on to become an England International.

In 1979 he took over the Youth Team and apart form a two-year stint as assistant manager to Lou Macari, has stayed in the job every since.

John is assisted by Adrian Riddiford, a teacher for 33 years, who is the Youth Scout and also handles the adminis-tration.

Boys are writing in for trials all the time hoping to become one of the 16 youths on the Club's books and Adrian handles all the letters. He has worked at the Club for two-and-a-half years.

John is happiest

working with the Youth Team.

"I became assistant man-ager at Lou's request, but I was glad when they let me return to manage the Youths. It's where my heart is," he said.

"I love to train them, and watch them play in the matches. The Youth Team job is the job I love the most. They are the Town's future, aren't they?"

John Trollope: "The youths are the Town's future."

The Youth Team with Adrian Riddiford, the Youth Scout, far right.

Don Rogers - Back to the future

Great players have come and gone down the years at Swindon Town. Harold Fleming, Harry Morris, Maurice Owen, Ernie Hunt. But perhaps one of the most admired is Don Rogers — scorer of two of the three goals for the Town which netted the League Cup 25 years ago in 1969.

Don is now manager of the Under 15s and trains Swindon's future soccer stars a couple of days a week. His appointment earlier this season has brought him into close contact with his former team mate John Trollope, Youth Team manager.

"John gets them after I have finished with them!" joked Don.

"The Town's Youth Team is the Club's future. But these young players represent the future for all clubs up and down the country.

"Investing in youth like this is not only a cheap way to get good footballers — but sometimes a way to get great ones."

Don should know. He joined the Town in January 1961 and was the Club's first apprentice professional. He stayed at the club throughout the 1960s, the high point of his career being the legendary 1969 3-1 win over Arsenal at Wembley.

The young players he now trains must dream that one day they, too, will play on the hallowed turf of Wembley.

With Don as their manager as well as their mentor, they have a better chance than most.

Wembley winner! Don Rogers scores at the 1969 Football League Cup Final, leading the Town to victory.

Khadija Buckland *is a public relations and advertising consultant and has worked on public relations campaigns for major companies, many in the Swindon area.*

She has her own company, Red House Media Services, and is also a freelance journalist, contributing features to national and regional newspapers.

Her first book, Arkell's Anniversary Album, was published by Red House last December. She is public relations and advertising consultant to Swindon family brewer, Arkell's.

Also available from Red House Publishing

The Arkell's Anniversary Album charts the history of this famous brewery, its pubs and the families that have been its backbone. It explains the secrets behind Arkell's beer and looks at the celebrations of its anniversary year.

Presented in an easy-to-read format with previously unpublished photographs, Arkell's Anniversary Album is available now from all good bookshops, Arkell's pubs or Arkell's Brewery at £4.99.